ESCAPE

DECIDE TO SURVIVE

JOHN DESHORE

NEXT WORLD

Escape

Decide to Survive

This is a work of fiction. Names, characters, organizations, places, events and incidents are either products of the author's imagination or used fictitiously. Any resemblance to actual persons, living or dead, events or locations is strictly coincidental.

First Edition May 2020

Next World

DEDICATION

To fathers who feel the burden of protecting their families.

1

FIVE LIVES

Aerospace engineer Dan Littrel filed out of the auditorium with the other 300 employees. They had just been briefed on the conflict in Kashmir. It would be business as usual at the company. Estimates that over twelve million people had been killed in the regional nuclear exchange were just beginning to roll in. He dialed his wife on the phone. She picked up and greeted him.

"Kate, it's time. Empty the safe deposit box."

"Are you sure?"

"Yep. They just told us that nothing changes. It was the same briefing we got from the morning news. They don't know anything we don't know."

"Dan, are you sure? It seems premature."

"Too soon is better than too late, love."

"Okay, I'll do it. On my way."

Kate grabbed her car keys and told Kyle, her son, that he was in charge for the next hour.

She drove to the bank where a long line snaked out the door and made her way forward, to the front of the line.

"I don't need a teller," she said to the young woman standing in front of the doorway.

She found a woman standing across the doorway.

"I can't let you in now, there are too many in the building. Fire marshal's orders."

Kate smiled at her, "I don't need a teller, just want to get to my safe deposit box."

The woman looked back into the bank. "Sure. Just wait for somebody to leave."

"Has it been like this all day?"

"Up to $200 is all we can do today. They are trying to avoid a rush on the bank."

Kate nodded in understanding. "Might be too late for that."

A few minutes later Kate exited the bank. The box was mostly empty, and the bag over her shoulder was heavy. She was trying to walk naturally but the 12-pounds made it difficult.

Kate thought how lucky they had been to put most of the cash in the box last week. She was shaking with nervousness. Her free hand slid down into her purse until she felt the reassuring cold olive drab metal of her Glock. She opened her trunk and lifted the heavy bag up and over its lip. It landed with a thunk. She shut it and looked around. Nobody was paying attention. She dialed her husband from the sun-scorched front seat.

"I have it. Is today the day?"

"Nope, we have more prep to do. Let's plan on the morning so we have all day to travel. How much gas you got?"

"Almost full. Stations are backed up right now, anyway. Round the corner."

"Okay, get home and stay there until I show up. Get everybody ready to go, just in case. Hey, honey, there is nobody I would rather have backing me up than you right now. Thanks for that. I love you."

"I love you too, Dan, but I am so scared."

"It'll work out for us. We've decided to be survivors. We are ready and have a plan," he assured her. "Talk to you later."

Ever since the bombing, the media was working night and day to scare the populace while the federal government worked to calm them down. Talk shows emphasized food shortages, transportation interruptions, growing war, nuclear winter and political instability. Angry protests had been breaking out for no apparent reason other than to oppose the increased police presence. More cops came because of the protesters. Dan unplugged the television a couple days ago.

As Kate pulled up to a traffic light, she saw another bank on the corner and people lined up outside. As her car idled at the light, an angry man emerged. He started yelling at the crowd and at the bank. A security guard standing off to the side moved over between him and the bank. The irate customer yelled all the more. The guard flicked the strap holding his gun in its holster. Immediately, and no more than fifty feet from Kate Littrel, she saw the angry customer try to grab the holstered gun. The guard was fighting for control of the weapon. Somebody behind Kate honked. She looked up and the light was green.

A shot rang out. Screams, then a thunder of people scrambling and shouting. Some hit the ground. Most ran for their vehicles. Kate stomped on the gas, and her car moved forward, leaving the mayhem behind. How did it end? She didn't see. Didn't care. Her heart was beating fast, and she was shaking. She was glad that her two boys and girl were safe back home.

As Dan eased out of the parking lot of United Aerospace, he noticed that the guards shouldered rifles. In ten years he had never seen more than a handgun. The crisis changed everything. He had to stop, waiting behind a car in front of him. He lifted the small hatch on the center console of his truck to see his handgun. He eased up on the brake to exit the outbound lane next to the guard shack. Handing over his ID, the guard scanned it by holding it up to a reader built into the side of the guard shack. A computer screen chirped. The guard studied its response then focused on the driver.

"Mr. Littrel, have a good day," the guard smiled. "Stay off the streets. It's getting dangerous out there. By the hour."

"Good suggestion." The guard handed Dan his ID. "Thanks."

This could be his last trip to the United lab. Nobody was aware. He knew today's meeting was a warning. As a defense contracting firm employee, he suspected that they might offer protection to the essential staff. A man with a wife and three children? Probably not.

Twenty-five minutes later, Dan pulled up into his driveway. Kate was home already. A strange orange light filtered down over his suburban house. He looked down the street at the orderly line of beige and brown houses. Dan sat for a moment in the driveway. How could they walk away from this? Unlike his wife's nervousness, Dan felt an excitement. A guilty pleasure. He had this.

He slipped the handgun into a waist pack and slung it over his shoulder as he got out of his truck. He was greeted by his neighbor, Bill Webber.

"Hey Dan, how are you doing?"

"Great, Bill, you?" Dan did not want to chat right now.

"I got a favor to ask. Any chance you could ask Kate to come over and check on Evie tonight? We're a little worried about her. We aren't supposed to go to the hospital unless it is an emergency."

Kate was a physician's assistant. From pains to sprains, she was known around the neighborhood as the best source of medical advice. Free.

"Sure, I'll ask her, Bill."

"Thanks. Watching the news is making us nervous."

"What is your plan for getting help if something goes south for Evie?" Dan knew the probable answer.

"Try an ambulance, I suppose."

"Listen, Bill, this situation is probably going to get much worse before it gets better. Don't rely on anybody but yourself for getting Evie to the hospital. Make sure you have gas and whatever you need to get there. We might not be around."

"Going somewhere, Dan?"

"We might be. Not tonight, though. Kate should be able to drop over," Dan evaded.

"What a mess this world is in, Dan. The damn politicians had better get this straightened out," he kicked a toy. "Before it's too late."

"Bill, the time for relying on politicians is over. But I got to get inside now. Look for Kate a little later." Dan was greeted by a pile of bags inside.

"Hey, where is everybody?" he called as he stopped to look at a stack of mail on the island in the middle of the spotless kitchen. There was a baseball glove on the kitchen table along with a frisbee.

Kate walked into the living room from the master bedroom. She gave him a hug.

"I saw a fight at the bank. The guard shot a mad man," she said.

"At our bank? That's too close."

"No, another bank. I'm fine. People are crazy. Poor man. Hope he makes it."

"But you're safe, right?" He hugged her and did not want to let go. He inhaled her coconut fragrance and stroked her hair.

"I'm fine. They aren't allowing withdrawals at most of the banks now so people are getting a little crazy."

"Are the kids all here?"

"The boys are upstairs playing video games. Sophie is over at Ann's."

"Can you get her home?"

"Right now? Is there a need?"

"I would just feel better if it is all the same. By the way, Bill wants you to check on Evie."

"Okay, after dinner. What are they going to do, dear? If...when this situation gets worse?"

"It'll get worse, and they will suffer," Dan replied gravely, "But we can't take care of them when we have our own five lives to worry about."

An alarm in the kitchen shrieked. Kate jumped. The emergency weather radio. It beeped long and loud for a few seconds.

"This is an emergency broadcast message. This is not a test. This is an actual emergency. There is a curfew going into effect at 9 pm this evening. All non-essential personnel must stay indoors from 9 pm until 6 am. Local law enforcement will take appropriate steps to ensure compliance. Essential personnel includes emergency responders, fire, police and medical personnel. A failure to comply with this curfew may result in arrest and detention. Thank you for your cooperation." The beeping resumed. Dan hit a button to silence it.

Dan looked at Kate and shook his head.

"In the morning, Kate, we move to the *Caruso*."

2

THE CARUSO

The *Caruso* was a 54-foot catamaran that Dan had seen on the front page of the *Miami Herald*. During one of Florida's hurricanes, the surge carried the boat across the roadway to rest in the parking lot of a Winn-Dixie. A salvage company had begun to remove her when Dan showed up with his checkbook in hand. He became the owner of a dismasted sailboat, stranded on the pavement.

Dan arranged for a crane and a large flatbed truck to tow her to a salvage yard. A marine inspection revealed no structural damage but there was a hole punched in the port hull and a lot of rigging was missing. Dan crudely patched the hole and had the boat towed to the water, pushed her in and hired another captain to pull her north.

They ended up at Merritt Island in the shadow of the John F. Kennedy Space Center. Dan rented two bays at a small industrial center a few blocks from the Indian River Intracoastal Waterway in Melbourne. They hauled the catamaran onto barrels in what Dan would call "the warehouse."

After a few weeks of research, Dan and Kate made seemingly endless lists of work to make her seaworthy. There would be a complete overhaul of the interior finishes and staterooms. Storage lockers, rigging and engines were on the list, plus paint, deck hardware and electronics. Altogether there was a good start to a live-aboard cat, yet the work was overwhelming. Dan would drive out Thursday afternoons, stay the weekend, and return to work on Monday morning. They made another step toward life on the water by selling their home and downsizing into a rental house.

Dan and Kate's dream was to work for two or three more years. When the kids were just old enough to appreciate it, they would put their lives on hold and sail the world until they ran out of money or grew tired of the seafaring life.

He was an engineer, his wife was medically trained. They could both homeschool their kids and the education would be like nothing else available.

Dan first heard about "the survivor's decision" at work. United Aerospace conducted a scenario planning seminar for all mid-to-senior level engineers. They developed contingency plans around company survival. How would a global pandemic affect the company? Its customers? Employees? Shareholders? What would happen in the event of a nuclear war? How would a failure of oil refining affect global production? What would happen if a rogue terrorist organization took out the US government? What if global climate change spirals out of control? What about an invisible flu pandemic, spread by talking and shaking hands?

At first, this all seemed like a fantasy to Dan, but he soon recognized a thread running through all the scenarios: United Aerospace was seriously planning for a breakdown of civil society.

No matter which scenario they played out, the reaction of most people was the same. Some waited for the problem to be solved by somebody else. Somebody who was not coming. Others took the initiative to survive. Most people expected systems of government, health care, food distribution, energy grids and other services to "just work." When they failed to do so, the rapid collapse of society was deadly.

A motivated few renegades took over and made life difficult for the rest, most of whom would perish.

At the end of the scenario sessions, a lecturer stood on a stage and put up one slide with a simple question: "Are you going to be a victim or a survivor?" He called it the survivor's decision.

Dan realized that surviving this collapse was easy for the single 20-year-old male. Hundreds of them worked at his company. Dan had a wife and three kids in tow. How could he possibly see them through the period of time United Aerospace called "Phase 3?"

Phase 1 referred to the immediate crisis. In Phase 1, people generally looked out for each other as a sense of camaraderie took hold. There was the expectation that law and order would be restored soon.

In Phase 2 people turn on one another as it became apparent that nobody was able to restore the peace and law. The strong would take advantage of the weak. Just a few would be prepared, armed and ready to face the changing crisis.

In Phase 3, mobs run rampant until the government exerts control through force. Federalization, or government takeover of communication, transportation and production would erode civil liberties. Militias and other nonconforming groups would be brought to heel. This period could be swift, or it could drag on if the resistance was well organized. Government forces cannot be everywhere and their primary objective is their own continuity. Where the government cannot enforce order, survival would depend on one's own resourcefulness.

In Phase 4 a new normal begins, as governments, businesses, institutions and people all attempt to reconstruct the former society.

As Dan turned wrenches and sanded fiberglass on the weekend a plan emerged. Regardless of the scenarios presented by the company, a live-aboard sailboat offered his family a lot of options. The more self-sustaining they could be, the longer they could stay at sea, the better off they would be. The ocean had fish, islands had water and vegetation. The wind was free and the boat could remove the family from the urban environments filled with dangerous people.

He shared this with a skeptical Kate who, after questioning, went along with her husband knowing that to oppose him was futile. When Dan got an idea between his teeth, no amount of pulling could yank it away.

Dan began to rework his catamaran design around the idea of survival, beyond pleasure cruising. Instead of a standard turnbuckle he installed a heavy duty turnbuckle to keep tension in lines. He strengthened the engine mounts. He installed a complete solar energy system. The Yanmar diesel engines had complete backup sets for parts known to fail. He stowed extra yards of steel cable for masts. He strengthened chain plates, which held the rigging to the fiberglass inside the hull. He enlarged the gas tanks. Dan filled otherwise wasted space with water bladders and storage lockers. Shortwave, marine and military radios were added. Two small generators were fit into the engine compartments, one in each hull.

All around, the boat was hardened for years at sea. It became Dan's obsession. Friends and family began to talk about when the boat would hit the water as the "one to two years" turned into "four to five years."

And then there were the guns and ammunition.

Dan stockpiled bullets. He settled on a standard 9-millimeter size along with 556 rounds for the rifles. He bought ammunition as each paycheck would allow. He canceled his retirement contributions and plowed the savings into brass and gunpowder. He built a hidden wall with a room at the workshop and began filling it with ammunition and bought AR-15s, handguns and tactical gear to go with them.

They would not take all of this ammunition and firearms with them on the water. Some were intended to be the currency to buy final supplies such as fuel and perhaps assistance in getting the boat in the water, for barter or whatever the situation might demand.

He taught Kate, Kyle and Cooper how to shoot. They spent a few days each month at a gun range in east Orlando.

He began to buy gold coins and bars and store them in the bank deposit box. When that was full he kept them in their closet. Whatever he didn't spend on boat repairs, equipment, bullets and guns was turned into gold.

He found a couple of shipping containers and had them moved into his work area. He turned one into one big Faraday cage. This would protect the contents from an electromagnetic pulse. Should it come to nuclear war this cage would keep all electronics inside the cage safe. To each corner, he welded a cable with a long spike that was set deep in the ground. He welded a metal fence to the hinged edges of the doors to provide complete containment. The opening between the swinging doors had a piece of this fencing that was pulled over the door and secured when shut. Inside, he lined the container with plywood and sprayed expanding insulation on the ceiling so that no wall would come into contact with the contents. He built wooden shelving inside for the boat electronics, extra engine parts, handheld radios, and a couple generators. He added some marine appliances for the kitchen and a ham radio as well.

The other container was used for storage. It was divided into a deep storage area and an immediate access area. He only stockpiled a few weeks worth of food and no water. Instead, he focused on things he could trade. He purchased cases of cigarettes. He focused on tools and supplies that would make survival more likely. He had water purification kits, basic hand tools, rope of various types, extra sailboat parts and an array of utility oriented outfits for his whole family. His wife worked in health care. There was a medical kit which included antibiotics, painkillers, antiseptic, bandages, gauze, tape, sunscreen, masks, scalpels, gloves and other items.

All of this was located 48 long miles away from the suburban house they were renting.

3

CHECKPOINT

At 4 am Dan and Kate woke up and prepped for the day. Dan emptied the refrigerator, mostly into the garbage, and went room by room, locking windows. Their lease would end in a few months and Dan had dropped a check for the landlord in the mailbox the night before. They didn't have any special attachment to this rental house. Dan felt the chances of coming back were slim, but it could happen. They could start over with a new lease.

At 5:30 the kids were dressed and assembling around the kitchen table for breakfast. The stuffed garbage bags and empty refrigerator were not normal.

"What's going on?" fourteen-year-old Cooper asked.

"Today we move onto the *Caruso*," said Dan to his family, "and we aren't taking anything other than our go bags."

"What the heck?" asked Kyle, the oldest at sixteen years. "Why didn't you tell us before?"

"The situation around us requires that we act now," replied Dan.

"What about my friends? Don't I even get to say goodbye?" Kyle asked.

"I am afraid not. In fact, I need all the family cell phones when we are done here. We won't be using them for anything anymore. Kyle and Cooper, I am going with you to get the phones right after we eat..."

"Dad, this is crazy. Why are we the only ones who do stuff like this?" Kyle whined.

"You know why. We have a plan, other people don't. This situation may settle down in the next few days or weeks but it might not. If it does, we can come right back here. If it doesn't, any steps we take now are very important."

Kate, who had been silently listening, jumped in. "We have been dreaming about life on the water for a long time, now we are going to get our chance. Lots of people would love to be doing this. It'll be an adventure."

Her brothers did not share her enthusiasm.

"What else do we need to do, Dad?" asked Cooper.

"Next, we're going to lock down the house as if we were going on vacation."

"And?" asked Cooper.

"Then we load up both cars with whatever gear is left and drive out to the warehouse," said Dan.

Sophie, seven years old, chimed in about her cat. "What about Rixie?"

"We are going to give Rixie a lot of extra food and let her outside. She always wants to be outside these days anyway," said Kate. She hugged Sophie, who made a disappointed whimper. "Cats know how to survive. If we come back, she'll be here. If we don't, she will be just fine."

Sophie looked at her mom as her eyes brimmed with tears and a dubious expression filled her face.

"Don't worry about her, honey. Rixie is a survivor."

"Just like the rest of us," said Dan, "let's get ready. We want to be on the road at 6 when the curfew lifts.

After a silent breakfast, the kids went to their rooms to get their bags. Dan followed the two boys and took their phones. He returned to the garage and was loading the truck.

Dan handed Kate a map. "No more phones, babe. I know it

sounds paranoid, but we are best off if nobody knows what we are up to. I don't think it will matter in a day or two but until we are out of the port, we should be careful."

"Sure," she said. She was never one hundred percent on board with all of Dan's preparations, but the shooting yesterday showed her how violent strangers could be so close to home. There was no harm in being ready. *Living at sea is our dream and plan anyway,* she told herself. They are behind schedule on that dream.

"We'll take the usual route. Me in the truck. You follow in the car. I need you to follow very close. I don't want anybody to get in between us," he said sternly, "We need to take this situation very seriously."

"Okay," said Kate, "drive so I can follow you."

"Where's your gun?" asked Dan.

"In the outside pocket of my bag, on the passenger side floor of the car."

"Perfect. Make sure you got a full magazine. Do you have your permit and papers ready?"

"We went over this. Of course, I do," she replied with a slight glare.

"Okay, turn to channel 3 on the handheld. After a few transmissions, when I say *jump* we move to the alternate frequency."

"This seems over the top," Kate rolled her green eyes.

"Let's hope it is. And damn, Kate, those eyes are beautiful when you roll them at me." He smiled. She flipped him a look that said *whatever.*

Kyle joined Kate, and the two younger kids rode with their dad. The garage door went up and they headed out onto the street. Nobody even looked back. The rental never felt like home to any of them anyway.

They lived just south of the Orlando International Airport and planned to drive to 192 and then head east to Melbourne. Being this far east, they would not have to pass by the gaudy tourist attractions of Kissimmee or the theme parks which made Orlando what it was. Dan looked up in the sky and did not see any commercial air traffic.

With almost fifty million passengers a year passing through every year, this struck Dan as odd. His mind drifted to the tourist economy of Central Florida. *What a great time to get out of Mouse Town while they still could*, he mused.

About a mile later they turned south on Florida SR 15. Ahead of them they saw a mix of flashing lights and traffic was backed up. They pulled to a crawl and noticed that people were being stopped. Dan prepped his ID and grabbed the radio.

"Get your ID ready. I'll hide this radio, you do the same," he commanded as gently as he knew how.

"Okay," came the one word reply.

Sophie sat silently in the back seat among suitcases fighting sleep.

As they approached the checkpoint, Dan observed the setup. Two sheriff's cruisers were parked across the road. Another two flanked those on each side, making passage around difficult. Cars were being checked and most were being directed to turn back. Dan swore under his breath.

As he pulled up, his window was down and his ID was ready. He had his hands on the wheel but his fingers were pointed up with his ID between the index and pointer fingers of his left hand.

"Officer, good morning." Dan looked at the officer's badge and name tag, taking note of both.

"Where are you headed, sir?"

"Melbourne. Why do you ask?"

"Only essential traffic is allowed. On what business are you traveling to Melbourne?"

"Personal business, sir, it isn't martial law now is it?" Dan's tone was respectful.

"No, it is not," replied the officer, "but there is a lot of restlessness and we want people to stay safe."

"Is Melbourne dangerous?"

The officer chuckled. "No. Let me see that ID, please. Give me a minute." The officer took Dan's ID back to one of the squad cars.

Dan looked over at Cooper. "Just stay quiet. They can't do this and they know it. But we want to be good citizens, right?" Cooper just nodded in assent.

The checkpoint line grew longer. Dan knew the longer the line grew the more likely he would be allowed to pass.

"Please turn around and head back north, sir." The officer handed Dan his license.

"I am not going to do that, sir," replied Dan evenly. "Unless you can show me a legal reason, I have every right to travel where I want to."

"Sir, step out of the car, please." The officer's face hardened. He looked more alert and stared hard at Dan.

Dan stared right back. "Under what pretense?"

"Because I told you to, dammit." He said it softly but impatiently. He then spoke something into his microphone that Dan could not catch.

"Am I being detained?"

"No. Just step out of the car."

"Am I being detained, sir?" In his rearview mirror, he saw Kate behind him.

"No, you are not being detained. Will you please cooperate and step out of your vehicle?" Dan felt the energy in his demand rising.

Another officer walked up and asked a question which Dan could not hear. She studied Dan and then scanned down the long line of cars. Maybe a half-mile now.

"Sir, you can go through. Be careful out there." She gestured with her hand for him to move forward.

"Thank you, ma'am," he said with a respectful tone. "That's my wife and son in the car behind us. I can't go on without them. She is basically a doctor if that makes any difference."

"We will wave them through. Now let's get a move on," she said.

Dan put his car into gear and drove sharply to the right, threading his way through the narrow gap between the parked cars. He slowed to see the officers in a heated debate as the female officer swept her hand toward Kate, indicating she should go.

As they got back up to speed, Dan grabbed the radio.

"OK! That was our first checkpoint. There will probably be more. Remember, unless you give them a reason to stop you, they cannot detain you. Let's stick together."

"Copy that," said Kate.

In his mind, Dan debated having two cars instead of one. They could all fit in the truck if they had to but he wanted that car in case they had to barter with it.

4

192

At the end of Highway 15 they turned left onto 192, toward Melbourne.

Dan realized that the checkpoint had been set up on the road right before they left Orange County. Osceola County was different. It was more rural with fewer people, more cattle. Perhaps they would be able to make it to Melbourne without incident. It was starting to lighten up outside and Dan began to feel more confident.

They weren't even five miles down the road when, in the distance, Dan could see traffic stopped again. This time, there were no flashing lights. Dan radioed, "Let's pull over and talk."

This was not a traffic stop like the last one, with moving cars and red brake lights. Dan reached behind him and found his small monocular. Holding it up to his right eye while closing his left, he could see that people were milling around the cars as if they hadn't moved in a while and would not be for the foreseeable future.

Kate came up on the passenger side of the car. She stopped and looked into the back seat to check on Sophie who was now asleep. Then she gave Dan a look that communicated, "What's next?"

"I'll walk up there and find out what's going on." He got out and stretched his legs, taking the radio.

"You guys sit tight, OK?"

"Sure," said Kate, "keep your radio handy."

Dan held it up and checked it. He stuffed it into his left cargo pants pocket while jamming his handgun into his belt and pulling his shirt down over it.

Dan came upon an old sedan with an older woman sitting in the front seat, smoking.

"Hello, ma'am." said Dan. "Do you know why we aren't moving?"

"Yep, there was a shooting up there and they shut down the road," she said.

"Any idea when it might open up again?"

"Nope, no idea. Been here since a little after 6." she took a drag on the cigarette.

"Were these cars parked here last night during the curfew?"

"I suppose they were."

"Do you know why there was shooting?" he asked.

"Nope."

Dan moved forward. Somebody was asleep in the back seat of the next car so he kept going on. A twenty-something man was sitting behind the wheel of a late model Ford Mustang, listening to music with headphones on.

"Hey, excuse me," Dan lightly tapped on the rear fender of the car, "do you know what's going on?"

Just then a shot boomed out. It was pretty close. Dan dropped down below the cars. The Mustang driver took off his headphones and sat up, saying, "What the hell?" His head jerked to look at Dan, who was dropping down lower while holding up his empty hands to the man.

Voices, shouting, then another shot echoed. Three, maybe four young men ran from car to car. More shouts. The men stood still. One man on either side of the truck. Leaning in. Demanding something at gunpoint.

Whoever it was handed something through the window. They turned toward Dan and walked to the next car, looking in the windows and evidently finding nobody. They shuffled to the next car.

They were about fifteen vehicles down from Dan's position. Dan heard a pickup behind him start up.

Just then the door of the Mustang opened. The man stood up. Dan saw he was raising a handgun toward the group. He pulled the trigger. It was so close to Dan that he saw the shell being ejected, bouncing off the car's open door. In rapid succession there were more shots and Dan heard a bullet whiz by him. Dan hugged the asphalt. The Mustang driver was returning fire when Dan moved back and away, squatting while pulling out his own handgun. He ran.

The old lady was starting her car when Dan crossed in front of her and grabbed the passenger door handle and pulled. Locked. The window was down so he reached inside and opened the door. She began pulling away before Dan could get into position to sit down. His right leg caught under the door. She accelerated just as he pulled his leg in. She was staring straight at the gun in his hand. Dan had not meant to point it at her and he quickly repositioned.

"I am not shooting you," Dan said quickly. She veered off the road and then back on again. "Slow down. I just want to get back there to my family." He motioned behind them.

She continued to roll backward but under more control now. She hadn't said a word, just looked very annoyed.

"Thanks," Dan said, "just a little further and I'll get out."

When he turned to look behind he saw a shotgun on the rear seat.

"Get that shotgun up here in the front seat with you and don't stop for anybody. We'll try another way around and you might consider the same." He talked with a monotone voice, trying to calm her down.

She glanced through the rear window and continued in reverse.

"Okay, this is fine. If you stop, I'll leave."

She slowed down to a stop. Dan was glad to get out. More shots echoed as the sedan did a three-point turn and drove off drunkenly heading in the wrong direction in the eastbound lane.

Dan hustled back to their vehicles. Kate's window was down and he motioned for her to get out.

"We're ditching your car here. We can't be separated like this."

"What happened up there?"

"Some punks were robbing folks in the cars and somebody shot at them. A gunfight broke out," Dan replied softly. "Get these kids into the truck, babe."

Cooper and Kyle moved bags from the back seat into the back of the truck. The two boys climbed into the back seat with Sophie as best they could with the bags there.

Kate slid into the front passenger seat. Dan snagged a fuel siphon, punched the protective screen, then primed the bulb to drain the car into a plastic gas can. He was about to heft it onto the truck when Kate urgently said, "Somebody is coming."

He grabbed the AR-15 case and opened it. He brandished the gun high in the air as a car approached. He switched off the safety.

"Get on the other side of the truck, c'mon guys, move!" The kids piled out of the truck.

He moved toward the truck and knocked over the gas tank. Crouching behind the truck, Dan saw that gas was spilling on the road now, vaporizing from precious fuel to pollution and running down into the ditch about 15 feet away. Dan glanced down warily. There were dangers everywhere.

The car rolled toward them then and swerved into the grassy median onto the westbound lane. A hand came up out of the window, empty and waving back and forth. A one-finger salute. Dan took a deep breath as he realized they were fleeing like most everyone else.

He slung the gun to his shoulder and quickly grabbed the hose out of the can, saving whatever gas was left. He capped it and placed it in the truck bed.

"Let's just go," he said.

"Dad, are we just leaving our car?" asked Sophie as he turned the ignition switch, grateful that there was no accompanying explosion.

"Yes, honey, we are. Better that we stay together in one truck."

"I am going to miss our car," she said with a pout.

"Me too," said Kate smiling at her. "She was a good car for us."

Kate turned and moved her purse from the middle of the back seat between the kids to the floor, where Sophie's legs weren't able to reach. She caught Sophie looking at her. Kate wondered to herself, *What will this little girl's future be like?*

5

CONFRONTATION

Dan swung the truck around and went down in the grassy median to head back on the west lane.

"We will go north at Nova Road and try to hook up with 520," he said

They rode in silence. The sun was up now and it was getting bright but the light was different. A golden haze cast an unnatural and eerie light. Dan reached down to squeeze Kate's hand.

"We'll make it," he said. "We are just going to be more careful."

Kate said nothing but looked ahead as a tear rolled down her cheek. Dan could feel her hand shaking.

He noticed his own exhaustion yet realized how amped and edgy he was. The adrenaline rush was gone and the brain fatigue was setting in. He took a deep breath and let it out. They passed a small group of people walking along the road and another car speeding over 70 in the eastbound lane.

"Did you see anybody get shot, Dad?" asked Kyle.

"No, I didn't, Kyle. It might have happened, but I didn't see it. We have to be ready for anything, but remember, we're the good guys. Don't let those people influence you to act like them. There are a lot of scared people out there and they do things they wouldn't normally do. We'll mind our own business and get to the boat. We are going to be ready."

"How long are we going to be gone for, Dad?"

"I don't know, but we should all be thinking that we are in this for the long haul."

The car fell silent again as the all-terrain tires hummed along at 60 miles per hour. Dan slowed and turned onto Nova Road and was soon back up to speed again. After ten minutes they were out in the midst of Deseret Ranch, one of the largest landholdings in the country. Dan felt a sense of safety being out here in the middle of nowhere where alligators and snakes lived. There wasn't another car on the road. They passed foraging cattle and swampy fields, palm trees and the occasional buzzard feasting along the side of the road.

A dark smudge in the sky indicated a fire somewhere ahead. The curves in the road made it impossible to tell if the fire was on the road or off to the west in the hammocks and scrub. Dan instinctively slowed down. Kate glanced over, brow furrowed, eyes still red.

"Do you think it's a problem?" she asked.

"It might be," he said, "until we get closer, we won't know."

They had slowed to 45 miles per hour as Dan tried to analyze the situation. He estimated they were within a mile and a half of the source of the smoke, but it was clearly up and around a bend in the road. As they cleared the curve, they saw a doublewide trailer now smoldering down to its steel chassis. In the front yard were a couple of cars and somebody was laying face down on the front steps.

"Oh my," said Kate. "What happened here?"

Dan punched the accelerator.

"This thing is bringing out the worst in people," he said, "it's sad."

"Nothing has even happened here in the US," she said. "There is no war here, no food shortage. What the hell is happening?"

"All of the arrangements we had with each other, as people, as a society, are being broken. The day they froze the stock markets people figured out that there are new rules. Fear is causing some people to revert to the worst version of themselves. Hey, we knew this was a possibility, and we are going to be fine. Let's stick to our plan and get on the water. We can sit the worst of this out and do a little exploring as we go."

"I hope so."

"I gotta go pee," a small voice said from the back seat.

Dan chuckled. "Civilization as we know it is coming to an end, but Sophie has to take a pee!"

Cooper laughed and said, "Some things don't change, no matter what else does."

They all felt lighthearted for a moment. Dan slowed down as they approached the stop sign for the 520. He braked. A couple semi-trucks blocked the road, east and west. A makeshift checkpoint caused the traffic clog. Dan spotted men with weapons milling about the trucks. Dan stopped the truck and threw it in reverse, backing up quickly toward Nova Road.

A battered van broke across the road behind Dan, forcing him to brake hard. He came to a full stop. As he looked up, a man with an enormous gray beard, a bulging gut and a baseball cap with a Florida Gators logo stepped up from the ditch. He was raising a rifle from his hip. Dan's hand shot down, grabbed his Glock, and raised it to the window. The two men were locked onto each other.

The bearded man yelled, "Get out!"

Dan shook his head back and forth and pushed down the button to drop his window.

"No, sir, we are not getting out. Put your weapon down, and I will too," Dan replied evenly.

"Don't be a dead man. Get out of the damn truck."

"Check out your rearview mirror," the bearded man said with a smile spreading across his face.

Dan didn't take his eye off the man. From the back seat Kyle said, "Another one coming up behind us, Dad. My side of the truck."

"Get out. We got the jump on you."

Dan's mind raced. The truck did not matter. Probably a liability at this point. The gear mattered a lot. What would they do to his wife and kids? He inhaled for an answer and was preparing to lower his gun knowing he had no choice. The rear door handle popped on the passenger side. He could hear the door opening. He knew he had lost.

Bam! Dan jumped in his seat. He turned around and saw smoke curling up from Kate's Glock, neatly folded into Cooper's hand. For a second he froze. The man standing outside the back door crumpled backward like a marionette with no wires. Dan swiveled his head back around but his finger squeezed before his eyes could catch up. His gun bucked in his hand and for the second time in a brief moment the roar of a gun in the truck cab stunned their ears. He felt the sting of gunpowder on his face as a shell ejected against the windshield.

The bearded man's head turned in a wide arc, blood spraying and his arms rising as the gun fell. Dan squeezed another shot. The roar at close range was like a hammer on the ears of the Littrel family. Dan slammed the truck in gear and they sped back down Nova Road as the rear door swung shut.

6

OVERLAND

Stunned, they hurtled back down the road.

Dan punched the steering wheel and yelled. The kids stared ahead, expressionless. Dan inhaled, exhaled and then forced himself to breathe evenly.

He just shot a man. His son just shot a man. He looked over at Kate who was weeping, her head in her hands.

Dan tried to ignore her for the moment and think. They could not use US 192 or 520. There were other options, all in the wrong direction. They would have to drive back to where they had just come from. He wondered if the two dead men had been coordinating with others and if somebody would be sent after them. What was their next step? What gave them the best path for survival? His mind raced but conclusions were elusive.

The silence was broken only by Kate's subdued weeping. Dan struggled between telling her to stop so he could think and showing empathy. A few minutes passed as they drove directly south.

"I am sorry, Mom," said Cooper in a small voice from the backseat.

Kate sobbed harder. Dan reached back with his right hand until he found his son's knee. He gave a squeeze and said, "You saved our lives, Cooper. You have nothing to be sorry about. When evil people try to harm your family, you take action. That's all you did."

They were passing a tall radio tower, on the right. Ahead of them he began to see a car, not a truck, painted green coming at them in the opposite lane. Dan slowed instinctively, then pushed the pedal down until he was pushing 80 mph. As the vehicles approached, Dan saw that it was actually a line of Humvees, four in military green and desert tan.

From the backseat, Kyle asked, "Dad, is that the Army?"

"I think so," Dan replied soberly.

They whipped by in succession and Dan eased off the gas. He watched in his rear view mirror and, when they were a mile or so past, he saw their brake lights come on. It suddenly dawned on him that they were pulling over by the radio tower.

"I think the Army is going to guard the radio tower," said Dan out loud. "Which is pretty smart."

They would soon approach the bend in the road, forcing them back to the west. Dan slowed. At the elbow, he took a smaller road which kept them going south.

"We are going to head as far south on Deer Run Road as we can, and then walk the rest of the way."

"We are going to walk? In the swamp?" she asked, her crying abruptly stopping.

"It's about 12 miles from here to I-95 but we'll have to walk. The ranch lies between us and Melbourne. Our truck is too attractive a target and we don't want to be around people right now. It's isolated out here."

Kate wanted to argue. She imagined going back to their house to ride it out like her neighbors were doing right now. The thought of traversing a swamp made her dread the next few days. The heat, the mosquitoes, the snakes, and all the other dangers made her want to say no to her strong-willed husband. The trauma of the last 24 hours had taken the fight out of her.

"How long will it take us to cross?" she asked.

"It depends a lot on what we find. We have to cross the St. Johns at some point," Dan said, "and we might find trails. We might not. Best case, we can do about 4 to 5 miles a day. Worst case, we will cover a mile if we get caught in really wet ground. We have gear and we'll be careful."

Dan slowed down as he neared the turnoff and elbow. The truck bucked a bit as they went down over the lip of the road onto the gravel of Deer Run.

"This is an active ranch and they won't want us driving through here. Those cattle are going to be worth a lot of money now. We will have to turn off and try to hide the truck back in the woods before we get too far down the road. Even then, they will probably find it within a day or two," Dan was talking out loud as he thought through the next few days. He was lamenting the loss of the truck and the gas, but reminded himself that these were just tools to survival and were no longer serving a purpose.

"This is it," he said, "we are going to leave the truck in the woods somewhere here."

He found a clump of trees across the opening and drove through spiky ground cover. The truck finally had to stop as the foliage was just too thick.

"Can you guys open your doors?" he asked.

Kyle opened his door and pushed it open. "Yep, no problem," he said.

"Everybody out. Grab your stuff. I got the gas," said Dan. "Kate, empty your purse." She followed orders without a word.

"Sophie, do you still have to take a pee?" Dan asked.

"Yes. Do I have to do it here?" she asked.

"Go around the front of the truck and lean back on the bumper. We won't watch," Dan said.

Dan had retrieved a heavy, square pack from the back of the truck. It had their gold coins in it. He strapped it on the front and strapped his backpack on his back. He put his handgun into his waist, stuffed under his belt. He put the strap to an AR-15 over his left shoulder and with his right hand he grabbed another rifle.

"You boys tote your pack and a rifle. I am taking your mom's rifle. Everybody should have a water bottle," Dan instructed.

"Can I take this extra water?" asked Kyle.

"If you can carry it, you can take it," said Dan. "It's going to be heavy."

Kyle picked up a 3.5 gallon water jug in one hand.

"I think I can manage it for a while," he said.

"Okay," replied Dan.

Sophie rounded the corner of the truck in a mock march and said, "I feel like a new woman!" with a big smile.

"Good job. From now on, you are in charge of peeing around here, okay?"

"Yes sir!" she said and made a salute.

Dan put the keys on the front seat and shut the door without locking it.

"Bye truck, said Sophie, patting the rear bumper. Dan gave her a quick smile and a wink.

Kate hefted her pack onto her back and they were ready to go. They were traveling lighter now, except for the heaviness of what had just happened and the premonitions of what was to come.

7

CAMP

It was about 10:30 in the morning and the sun ascended into a tropical Florida sky tinged purple, then azure.

Dan took out his GPS unit and turned it on. It featured a moving map and he was hopeful that it all worked as expected. He watched as the unit's satellite indicators lit up. The map display glowed, revealing their correct position. It was a topographical map. All it showed were the light green and blue patterns of swamp. They were glad to feel ground under their feet now, though, and they set off toward the east, toward the warehouse and their escape boat.

The going was rather slow. After about five minutes they stopped and dropped their packs, looking for insect repellent. Even in the heat of the day the mosquitoes were buzzing around them, particularly when they were under the tree canopy. The trees came and went as they marched on.

"We're making pretty good time," said Dan, knowing that they were not, in fact, making good time. He checked the GPS occasionally to make sure they were tracking in the right direction.

About 45 minutes in, Kyle announced it was time to drink.

"I can't keep carrying around this jug. It's just too heavy," he said.

They took a long drink, refilled their bottles, and then passed around the jug.

"The more we drink, the less we carry," observed Cooper.

"Nah," Kyle contradicted, "We are just carrying it somewhere else."

Cooper said nothing in return. Dan motioned for them to get moving again.

After another half hour of walking, the heavy chop of an Army Black Hawk helicopter broke the forest silence. Likely headed to Patrick AFB. They were mostly out in the open and had to backtrack when their way forward was blocked by large saw palmettos. Dan stopped them to point out the razor sharp stems.

At noon they stopped in the shade of a small sabal palm grove. Dan suggested they rest for the next hour, eat an energy bar from their back, and stay out of the sun for a while. In each backpack there was a small tarp. They pulled out the tarps and lay them on the ground. Dan had two, one for himself and one for Sophie. They sat in silence. Exhaustion had taken its toll, more from the events of the past days than the march.

Kate reached over and traced her hand along Cooper's hairline, moving his hair off of his forehead. He looked at his mother with the faintest of smiles and she returned the look. The air was moist and heavy, and Dan began to doze off.

Sometime later, Dan felt a kick in his side. Sophie had stretched out with her foot and was urgently nudging Dan. He sat up, immediately alert. Sophie pointed across the clearing. Something moved in the sawgrass brush. He grabbed a small monocular. The brush was moving and cracking, but then everything would go. Finally, a huge white steer with long, curving horns broke into the clearing. Dan exhaled relief. A cow stepped out and then, in the span of about a minute, six were grazing and then moving forward.

It dawned on Dan that it was the middle of the day, the sun was high and it was hot. Why would the cows be moving about at midday? Fear gripped him. He nudged Kyle and said in a low voice, "Let's get moving." Dan checked his weapon as they walked. The GPS showed they had moved in an almost straight line due east since he had first set course. They had covered a little over a mile and a half. What lay ahead?

Kyle, in the lead, suddenly stopped. "Lots of water ahead."

In front of them, stretching out for quite a while, was a marshy swamp. The muddy, almost rotten smell of decaying vegetation filled their noses. Clumps of spiky ground cover gave way to tall grasses. Dan lifted his foot and looked down. The boot print filled with water. He knew it would come to this sooner or later. They backtracked and then turned due south. They walked along a stand of sand pine, with thick needles covering the ground, making it easier to walk. They moved along as fast they could, but his family was tiring. Dan suggested a break. Packs hit the ground and soon everybody was sitting in silence, clutching a water bottle and wishing for air conditioning, home, or anywhere but here.

A sudden roar came upon them. They instinctively ducked an inch or two. As fast as they saw a squadron of military jets it was gone. A low altitude pass not far from where they were sitting. Dan looked at Kate and just stared back, too tired to respond.

"Patrick Air Force Base is just a few miles south of Melbourne. They sometimes fly out of there."

Kate just nodded slowly.

"Dad, what is going on?" asked Cooper. "Things have changed so fast."

"Well, we saw the signs and knew that things might get bad but I didn't expect this either, Coop.

"What signs?"

"I think the triggers were financial. As soon as people saw that the banks weren't able to give them their savings, they began to freak out."

Kyle chimed in, "People are stupid and they follow their emotions."

"Well," said Dan, "that might be true. But people rely on things to run the right way. Just the food supply alone is reason to be careful right now.

"Makes me hungry," said Sophie.

"Most grocery stores only have a few days of inventory. If these troubles interrupt food distribution, in about a week some people will be in serious trouble."

"Dad," asked Cooper, "what's our plan for food?"

"We have some stockpiled at the warehouse, but we're going to catch our own fish in the Atlantic and Banana River. Speckled trout, mangrove snapper, maybe a grouper or grunt. Certainly some blue crabs." Dan knew how much Cooper liked to fish. "And we can barter. We have supplies, so we can trade for what we need."

"All that stuff at the warehouse won't fit on the boat," said Cooper.

"You're right about that," said Dan. "We can hopefully come back and restock if we need to."

"How much longer? I'm getting blisters." Sophie interrupted. She was doing her best to keep up.

"We'll go for another two hours or so and then set up camp. How does that sound?" asked Dan.

"Great," she said with a little hint of a frown. "Let's get going, then."

Dan tousled her hair. "You are doing great."

He oriented his GPS. They started due east again, hopeful that the swamp didn't extend this far south. After about an hour, saw palmetto trees, razor sharp, blocked their way eastward. They tried to go around, only to find themselves in marshy ground, with water and mud making it impossible to proceed. They backtracked a couple hundred yards, toward a grove of pines. At this rate they would be lucky to make two miles. Discouragement was setting in.

"Let's set up camp, make a little food, and get to bed at sundown," said Dan. "Tomorrow we have to cross the St. Johns. Maybe in the morning."

They quietly began to get gear out of their bags. The adrenaline surge was giving way to feelings of overwhelming exhaustion. They found trees suitable for hanging their hammocks and put the straps up. Dan set up his tent as well as Sophie's, which were both in his bag. A couple of small alcohol stoves were set up and some noodles for macaroni and cheese were soon boiling. The only talk was when necessary instructions were needed.

Kyle and Cooper were soon began filtering water they'd found in a natural spring and had all of the bottles topped up again plus an extra container for the morning. The family ate their simple meal in the opaque darkness that followed sunset. They cleaned up and prepped for a night in the pines. The bags were strung up in trees so nothing was left on the ground for a roving black bear. Panthers were rare yet occasionally sighted this far north.

"How are we going to cross the river tomorrow?" Kate asked her husband.

"We're going to find a shallow spot and walk across," he said.

"What about alligators?"

"Kate. You know as well as I do that alligator attacks are rare. They won't bother us," Dan replied. "We'll be careful."

"It's not the gators we will have to worry about," said Kyle. Before his dad could cut him off he continued, "it's the snakes. Mostly water moccasins."

The family climbed into their hanging cocoons and Dan zipped them all in, getting into his own little cocoon last. Even though they were safe from mosquitos and anything crawling, they had new dangers on their minds. Dangers that they had never considered before.

8

DOG

His name was Maddox Pendleton, but everybody called him Dog. It started out as Mad Dog, but it was shortened long ago. He was a large man, standing six foot, five inches, and he had long curly black hair and a bushy beard. He was powerful but well-rounded as he approached his mid-thirties.

This morning, as he woke up, his left arm was stuck to the bedsheets with dried blood.

"Shit," he said out loud to nobody but himself when he tried to move, "what the fuck?"

He leaned up long enough to look down at his arm then collapsed back into his pillow. The events of last night came back to him slowly. At first, it was as if the whole night had been a dream. But no, it was not a dream. Definitely not a dream, he concluded. He had been drunk at 4. That he remembered clearly. He had been at Red's, a bar on A1A in Melbourne, with Jillian. She had given him grief for drinking too much too early. She was a bit more sober, so she drove her car home to his rented house, had sex, and she had left soon after to check on her mom. That would have been a great night if he stopped there, he laughed to himself. He returned to Red's. Because he lost his driver's license long ago, he was walking. He did not even make it to the causeway bridge when he sat down for a smoke.

Across the intersection he saw four young men in their mid-twenties, thin and hairy, talking in a gas station parking lot. One swung a baseball bat. As Dog watched, they pulled bandannas up onto their faces and walked into the gas station. To Dog's surprise, a middle-aged man came out seconds later, with his hands over his head, followed by two of the thugs. Baseball Bat Guy swung repeatedly, as the attendant tried to shield himself. He went down, probably dead before he hit the oily cement, his head smashed beyond recognition.

Dog just stared. The batter swung one last time.

"What the fuck?" Dog said loud enough for them to hear.

He got up and started across the street. He knew one of the men raiding the gas station. Richie was also a regular at Red's.

"Dude," Dog called, "what the fuck?"

"World is coming to an end, man, don't you watch TV?" Ritchie shouted out.

The only TV Dog had watched in years was over the bar, always sports.

A siren wailed a mile or so away. Dog immediately looked down the street and then back at Richie. Time to fly. Dog had spent a few years in prison. Cops were never his friends.

"Better roll, Richie, cops," Dog said.

"Watch this, man," said Richie. He walked toward the sidewalk, lifted his shirt and took a handgun out from his belt line.

As the police cruiser neared the intersection, Richie stepped out and aimed at the police cruiser.

Dog took a few steps back as fear gripped him. He could not afford to be an accomplice in a police shooting. It was happening so fast. The cruiser did not slow down but kept barreling forward.

Richie never pulled the trigger but swept around in a half circle to keep it pointed at the speeding car. The officer ignored this obvious crime scene.

"They don't care shit about us," said Richie. "They got more important things to worry about right now."

Dog was dumbfounded. "What the fuck, man?" he asked again, shaking his head, "is this for real?"

"Dude, the fucking world is coming to an end. They don't care about some shit-ass local gangbanger stealing from a gas station."

Dog flashed a broad, stupid smile. Still half drunk and a whole night of trouble in front of him.

"C'mon man, we are heading down the street, beating who we find, taking what we want."

The other two came out from the store and Richie introduced them all around. Their pockets were bursting with cash and each had a six pack in each hand. They looked down the street. No more than 100 yards away was a small grocery store. The man with the bat pointed and said, "Hot damn, I'm hungry. Let's go."

As they approached the store they noticed that it was closed. A couple of older men were boarding up the windows. Richie fired into the air, and then aimed at the two men.

"Is it worth it?" Richie yelled from across the parking lot.

From the corner of the store came a muzzle flash and Richie spun in a circle. He dropped to the pavement. Blood pooled. His sightless eyes aimed for the sky.

"That's a question you should be asking yourself," called a voice from behind the rifle.

Dog looked down and reached for Richie's gun. Another shot rang out. Dog felt somebody jab him in the elbow and was going to turn to see who it was. He realized he had just taken a bullet to the back of his left elbow. He lifted it up to see the damage. The arm seemed to move alright.

Picking up the handgun, he scrambled behind a car for cover. He found the man with the rifle standing in the open, as if he had won the battle. Dog slowly sighted him, aware that his senses were dulled by alcohol. He moved slowly and squeezed the trigger until the gun lurched in his hand. The first thing he felt was a stinging sensation on his right thumb. He had placed it over the back of the gun's rail. It had snapped back and bitten into his skin. Then he looked up and saw the rifle fall to the ground, the man grasping his neck. He tumbled.

Dog walked around the side of the car. He approached the writhing man with the handgun drawn and ready.

"Hey dude," he called to one of his new friends. "Give me that damn bat."

He exchanged the gun for the bat. "Keep it on him," he said.

Dog lifted the bat overhead. The man was gasping for breath, a portion of his throat exposed. The bat swung higher and then came down, crushing the man's skull.

"The world came to end for you tonight, asshole," said Dog.

Dog grabbed the gun back, handed over the bat and said, "Let's go."

The gang rolled into the grocery where they started by smashing cash registers. Dog grabbed a carton of cigarettes and then rushed back to the beer coolers. He guzzled a beer, snatched a twelve-pack off the shelf and started toward the front of the store.

The two other thieves were sitting on a bench by the cash registers. One kicked forward a shopping cart filled with junk food, beer and cigarettes.

"So, what now?" asked Dog.

"I don't know, man, but I do know that you had better get all stocked up while you can."

Dog nodded his head slowly in agreement in a moment of sobriety.

"Why is the world coming to an end?" he asked.

"I don't know, some shit war in Asia or something, but I can tell you that the cops don't care about us anymore."

If that is true, thought Dog, *then I am for sure going to get mine.*

Now, waking up this morning it suddenly flooded back to him like a flushed toilet overflowing. He slowly peeled the bed sheet from his wounded arm. He tried to shower off the memories and the blood from last night and did his best to clean the wound. He didn't have a first aid kit so he wrapped duct tape around some toilet paper and ripped some bandages from his bed sheet. "Where," he wondered out loud, "do rich people hang out?"

It came to him quickly. They hang out on the shoreline. On the coast rich people have big houses and big boats. That is where the money will be. Dog grew up sailing. He wanted a boat. A big boat. But first he needed a drink. A big drink.

9

TO THE RIVER

Dan lay awake in the dark. It was early, 5:17, and although the sun was no doubt already painting a portion of the purple sky, all was black at the foot of the pine trees where they slept. There was absolute silence. *Strange,* thought Dan, *no jets in the sky*. He was stiff from the hammock and eager to get moving. He carefully and slowly unzipped the mosquito fly on the hammock and poked his head out.

He was immediately welcomed by a whining noise in his ears, as the hungry bloodsuckers were waiting for him. *How do they always find your ears first?* He finished unzipping and slowly spun around as stealthy and quiet as possible. He reached into his pocket for a small bottle of repellent and rubbed some on his face and hands. And ears.

"First things first," he whispered and moved out from the base of the camp to find a place to urinate.

When he finished, he walked back toward the hammocks and a small voice said, "Did you just do what I think you did?"

Dan chuckled quietly, "Yes, Sophie, I did," he whispered.

"Can I get up too? Gotta go," she said.

"Sure," said Dan, "but be quiet."

He helped her unzip her hammock and picked her up. She hugged him and then he set her down.

From somewhere over his left shoulder he heard a footfall among the trees. Dan dropped down to one knee and held a finger up to his lips. Neither moved for a few moments when another step could be heard. Sophie wrapped an arm around Dan's leg.

Dan's handgun was in the bottom of his hammock. He closed his eyes for a moment and concentrated on listening. Another rustle, and then another. He contemplated sprinting to the hammock but could not tell how far away the sound was. In the darkness, Sophie whispered, "Dad, look!" as she squeezed him.

A large buck, tawny and muscular with a rack of antlers, stepped out from behind the trees, sniffing the coastal wind. A faint but perceptible breeze was blowing just enough to carry their scent away but he still knew there was something not quite right. Dan stood still, a mere 15 feet from the buck. The deer took a tentative step forward. A doe stepped out behind him and then another. A small fawn walked into the clearing. The buck's tail was twitching now and his nose was bobbing up and down as he sniffed. He stamped once and in a moment bounded up and out of the clearing, the three others in pursuit.

"Wow, Dad," said Sophie, "they were so close."

Dan relaxed and smiled, "Yep, honey, they didn't smell us because the wind was blowing our way." He grinned at her, "I'll get some water boiling while you take care of your business. Don't go far."

Soon, water was heating up. Sophie came back to stand close to him.

"Be careful about fire ants," he said.

Kate's bag unzipped and she climbed down. She walked out in the woods for a few minutes before returning to a warm cup of instant coffee. They shared enough sunlight now to see each other's faces. It was moist and if there had not been a breeze there would certainly have been a fog.

"Hey boys, get up, oatmeal is about ready," Dan whispered with some urgency. He held up a couple packets of flavored instant oatmeal for Sophie to pick from. A few minutes later, they were all standing with cups of oatmeal. There was even some instant orange drink. As they packed up camp and began heading due east through the pines Kyle asked, "How long are we walking today?

"Well," Dan said as he considered the question, "it's probably going to take a couple hours to get to the river, then we cross it, and a couple more to town."

"I am sore already," said Kyle as he used his free hand to indicate the strap on his backpack.

The sun was now hitting the tops of the trees. Kyle was in the lead when he turned to say, "Stop. Swamp in front of us." Dan pulled out the map again.

"There are some canals cut in here and I think that is what we are looking at right now," said Dan. "Let's track north a bit and see if we can find the end of it."

Sophie shrugged and Kate gave her a defeated smile. Dan wondered if he could get his wife to the side for a conversation. She was not herself.

They turned north and marched for about 20 minutes along the rough edge of what appeared to be a long-forgotten man made canal. It joined up with another one, clearly cut and not natural.

"We'll wade through it," said Dan. "Let me go first and see how deep it is."

Dropping down into the water, his feet began to sink up to his thighs.

"It's really mucky," he said, "keep your feet moving."

The water climbed almost to his waist. He held his two rifles high and came up the opposite bank. He dropped his backpack and the rifles and came back across.

"Let's go." He hoisted Sophie up on his shoulders.

Cooper got about halfway across and slipped, putting one arm down and only his head was up.

"Don't worry about it, Coop," said Dan, "pretty soon we'll all be wet. Like you."

They emerged from the canal on the other side and Dan put his pack back on.

"Straight east now. We're already in the conservation area and the river is up ahead," said Dan. "It isn't very wide up ahead, but we can follow it south to a spillway. That's where we should find a road and it'll be easier to walk then."

They slogged forward. The pace was not much different than the day before. There were plenty of saw palmetto and marshy areas where they could not go forward. They stopped for an early lunch around 11.

Dan pulled out the GPS and held it up. After a few seconds it registered that they had only made about a mile in the past four hours. At this rate they would barely make the river before nightfall.

"How far?" asked Kate.

"You really want to know? A little past halfway there," he said.

"So, another night in the swamp," she said.

"Romantic, eh?"

Just then it dawned on Dan that he had a shortwave radio in his pack. He pulled it and lifted up and said, "News."

He pressed the scan button.

"This is a required emergency announcement. This notice will be read every fifteen minutes. A state of emergency has been declared. The US government advises all citizens to stay indoors. A curfew is in effect from 9 pm to 6 am. Until further notice, only essential emergency responders are allowed on roads during the curfew. Daytime travel is also restricted in some areas. Contact law enforcement if you need emergency medical treatment. Law enforcement has been authorized to use deadly force. This has been an official emergency announcement."

Dan looked at Kate, who stared straight ahead into space.

The announcer continued, "We have more local incident reports for you. On the intersection of Dean Road and Curry Ford Road there is a shooting reported. On South OBT and Locust there is a vehicle on fire. Maitland Avenue, all lanes are blocked." Dan clicked off the radio.

"We made the right call." He stood up to repack his bag.

10

KILLER

Dog knew where the big houses were. He had mowed their lawns and fixed their sprinklers.

He was headed there now, walking down the causeway, arms swinging wide and thinking about the end of the world. He felt retrospective, a feeling he didn't exercise often. He thought about his family and wondered what they were doing right now and what might become of them. He caught himself welling up with emotion. He was about the worst son he could imagine and guilt hit him hard. He tried to think about something else but his mind wandered back to his parents and their grief over him. His dad could barely express emotions on a good day, and the many bad days that Dog had created were tough on the old man. He thought about his mother, crying. *Stop it,* he told himself.

Then he remembered last night. He had committed violence before but this was something different. He swung that bat and hit that man so hard it killed him. Why had he done it? The world's coming to an end, he thought, who cares? Then he felt guilty all over again. He grabbed his cigarettes and lit one up. He would have to steal a few more soon.

"Damn," he said upon remembering there was a whole carton

back at the apartment. His thoughts were scattered and he shook his
head to clear it. He picked up his gait on the downhill section of the
causeway bridge.

"I am taking what I want," he said out loud to nobody but himself.

The words were hollow, even to Dog. His mind searched for something positive as guilt touched him again. Jillian, now she was good. In
Dog's hardscrabble life, Jillian was always there for him. He was 21 when
they first met. He had already spent two years in prison, released early
for good behavior, rehabbed and then he started drinking again. She
was a stripper, one of the finest and friendliest at The Playhouse. After
two visits, he was her infatuated regular. Pretty soon he was picking her
up after work and they became a couple. They had been together ever
since, although the definition of "together" varied. She would move in
and then out. Dog almost killed a customer one night who had grabbed
her boobs and forced himself on her. When he went to jail for it she was
his only link to the outside world. When he was court-ordered into
rehab, she came to family nights. She left The Playhouse when he got
out because it was just too hard for him. She was almost 30 years old
now, anyway, and tips were going to younger girls anyway. She got a job
as a waitress in a local diner. He'd sit for hours, nursing cold coffee at a
booth, watching her work. They fought and she moved out, only to
return again. He hit her once, and she left with a black eye, swearing
never to return. Dog thought that was the end but a few weeks later she
came back. In his whole life nobody had stuck with him like Jillian. In
his prison-tempered worldview, he owed her and he knew it.

She's good he thought to himself, *she always does the right thing.*

He thought about how she was taking care of her mother who
was dying of lung cancer. *Damn, I don't deserve her.*

He reached the end of the bridge and turned south on N Riverside
Drive. *This is where the money lives*, he chuckled to himself. The big
houses, he knew, were mostly facing west toward the mainland and
the million-dollar sunsets. The Atlantic side was mostly solid stacks
of timeshares and hotels, 15 stories or more. As he walked by drive-
ways he remembered landscaping projects that he had completed

along this road. Hot days and little pay to dig holes, plant trees, move dirt and take shit. He came to a stop in front of a gated compound. He had dug holes and planted palm trees here. A couple of Royals and a Sable. Those were his favorite, the Sables. There was no way to get a backhoe into the far corner of this lot so they had dug three huge holes by hand in the tropical summer heat. He would never forget that hellish job.

He climbed up onto the concrete and rock wall and looked in. The house was big, of course, and in the back, only half visible, was a large sailboat. *Whoa, a bug fucking boat!* he exclaimed inwardly. There was a big Lincoln Town Car in the driveway. The landscaping was impeccable. Of course it was, *I did that.*

He stared with satisfaction.

This is it. This is fucking it. I am going to watch the world end from here.

BEN THOMAS LOOKED in the refrigerator while the TV played loudly in the background. Ben was 77 years old and had been a highly successful real estate agent during the Florida boom years. Orlando had exploded from a small backwater orange grove town to the world's most visited destination during his lifetime. He had spent much of that time selling timeshares. It almost was not fair. His firm would offer discounts to Disney to those willing to sit through a simple presentation. Tourists arrived expecting to save a few dollars over the weekend and left spending tens of thousands over their lifetime.

But that almost felt like a previous life to Ben. His wife began to fail about ten years earlier. She had advanced Alzheimer's now and Ben had quit the office and devoted himself to her care. In the beginning, it was not bad because most of their friends had understood. Now, nearing the end, he was isolated and lonely. She was worse. He was gentle with her, remembering the hundreds of times she had put up with him and his long hours of weekend work. She was all he had.

He had found a new joy in being there for her. He called it, "My long march of love."

She did not respond to him anymore when he spoke to her. Their dog, Molly, had died about four months ago. Molly was attentive and he had been speaking to both of them in the monastery-like silence of the house. When the veterinarian said that Molly was suffering and it would be a mercy to put her down, Ben had cried like a baby. He wasn't proud of it, but he also wasn't ashamed. Molly had been a joy, riding on their golf cart through the neighborhood, relishing car rides and just being there. Now, Claire got all of his spoken words. And she didn't talk back either.

Ben thought about his son in Minneapolis. They had not spoken in about a week and every time he called he had gotten a voicemail greeting. The last time his son visited with his wife and two kids they had implored Ben to sell the house and move into something more manageable. The only memories Claire retained were in this house. If they moved she may lose those too. Now, she did not even retain those memories but Ben was too overwhelmed with her care to move.

Occasionally she would have a moment of clarity. Their eyes would meet and he knew that she knew that he loved her. That was all he wanted or needed from her now. They had a caregiver coming to the house but she had not shown up for a couple of days. She brought the groceries. Now, looking into the refrigerator, he realized that they were out of food and he might have to make a trip out or find somebody to deliver something.

"You can sure eat, girl," he said rather loudly so she might hear in the next room. "I better see what I can do to get somebody in here with some groceries."

He thought about calling his son. He was busy, though, and Ben didn't want to bother him.

Just then the house went silent, the ever-present hum of the air conditioning shut off. Ben looked up and the light in the refrigerator was dark too.

"Power's out," he called to his wife.

He closed the refrigerator door and shuffled into the living room.

Claire sat in her easy chair. Her head lay down on her chest as she slept soundly, bent forward. Ben gently placed a pillow behind her head and slowly eased her back in the chair. He pressed the release on the chair and moved it back to recline. She had a long trail of saliva running down her chin and he wiped it off. She was not dressed for the day. He could not manage that alone and he was grateful that she was mostly clean.

Ben thought he heard the front door. He twisted his head around to expose his good ear toward the source of the noise. He heard nothing and so assumed it was nothing.

"I am going to make some phone calls, Claire," he said softly. She didn't wake easily so he talked to her even when she was sleeping.

He went down the long hall toward their bedroom and found the telephone plugged into the charging cord next to the bed. He picked it up and pressed the power button. It lit up in his hand. He began walking down the hall back to the living room when he heard a fumbling noise. He quickened his pace. He was expecting to find that Claire had fallen out of the chair. That would be disastrous. He turned the corner into the living room.

A man with a bandage that wrapped most of his left arm was towering over Claire. He held her head in his arms and her head was twisted in an unnatural way. The man spun around toward Ben, letting Claire fall to the shag carpet. Claire reached out, her hands like claws, grabbing nothing.

"You can't do that!" yelled Ben. He started toward Claire when a fist came from nowhere and hit him square in the face. Ben fell back against the wall and slid down to his knees. He saw stars. His nose felt like it had been pushed into his forehead. Eyes flooded, he was blinded. The iron taste of his blood mixed with the salt and mucous.

"You don't remember me, do you?" asked Dog. He paused a moment and then shouted, "I dug holes in your fucking backyard!"

Dog stepped forward and threw a tremendous uppercut to Ben's stubbly chin which was at Dog's waist level. Ben's head snapped back and punctured the drywall. He slumped forward to the floor. Dog stomped on his head using the heel of his thick leather sandal. A red puddle grew around Ben's head almost immediately. Dog then stomped on Claire. She said nothing. He said plenty.

"Fuck!" he yelled, "I am Dog!" He stood there for a few moments breathing hard and looking around the room.

He threw open the door of a built-in closet and opened the door. It was filled with VHS tapes and DVDs.

"Where do you keep the booze, old man?" asked Dog, expecting no answer just as Ben had expected none just minutes before.

Dog searched from room to room until he found the liquor cabinet in the kitchen next to the sliding glass doors. He rattled bottles until he found whiskey. He pulled out the bottle, unscrewed it and gulped. Again. And again.

A childlike noise was coming from the living room. Dog stomped back in to find the old lady laying on the floor, with one arm waving in the air. Dog took four steps and looked down at her.

Vivid tragedy looked back up and for a second, Dog could swear she was trying to say something to him with those clear, blue eyes. What was it? She would not say it. He would not hear it. Meet your maker.

Dog placed his sandaled heal on her neck and stepped down. She grasped at his leg weakly and Dog pushed down harder until her neck crunched. She went limp.

Still holding the bottle in one hand, he turned to look out the glass doors.

"That is not just a sailboat," he said, "it's a fucking catamaran."

He took another swig. He knew a lot. He knew that he would soon be shit-faced drunk.

11

RIVER

They walked in wet pants and the day began to take on the same feel: sticky and uncomfortable. Kyle was slapping bugs and complaining. Cooper was more stoic than ever. Sophie's enthusiasm had given over to a blank face as she pressed forward. Kate plodded in silence. Dan, lost in his own planning, stopped abruptly.

"Time for a water break." They plopped down in a circle on a patch of sandy turf.

"How much further to the river?" asked Kyle.

Dan pulled out the GPS and waited for it to read the satellites. "As the crow flies, less than half a mile," he paused for a moment while studying the tiny digital map in his hand, "too bad we aren't crows, though, because we need to get a little further south before we cross."

"Nobody wants to be an old crow anyway," said Sophie as she stuck her chin up in the air and smiled.

"Nope," said Dan tousling her hair, "nobody does."

Dan flexed his arms and rolled his shoulders. His straps were beginning to wear on him and he was still carrying two rifles.

"We have to keep moving, folks, if we want to get to the movie on time."

He spoke with a smile, trying to lift everybody's spirits. It had the same effect similar statements made by dads throughout history had. None.

"When we get there, Dad, are we just going to sail?" said Cooper.

"First we have to load the boat up," said Dan. "It's far from the warehouse. Maybe we can sail her closer. I'm hoping that we can find a vehicle to borrow or barter for."

The boat had been floated for the first time about one month earlier. It was an ordeal which had included two forklifts, an oversize truck permit and some unhappy drivers who were stuck waiting for the catamaran to clear the road. Dan had taken them out on a short sail down the Indian River but he couldn't properly break in the boat and test the various systems. He was renting a dock at a private home about three miles from the warehouse over the Intracoastal causeway. He had been planning a short, week long shakedown cruise but now was just grateful the boat was in the water.

"Dad!"

Kyle was pointing toward the north. The whole family froze.

Two men were crossing the field to the north along a tree line. Both had rifles over their shoulders and were dressed for the bush, with boots and camouflage jackets. Their faces were painted green. One wore a baseball cap flipped backward and a pair of night-vision goggles pushed up high on his cap. The other wore a straw cowboy hat scrunched low. They both toted backpacks and walked alert and quickly.

Dan motioned for the family to slowly lower themselves and they froze, Dan taking a knee.

"Just be still," whispered Dan. He set one of the rifles down on the grass and rested the other on his thigh in a ready position.

They watched from a long distance as the pair cut a straight line to the east coming within 75 feet of them. The men did not slow as they passed and everyone breathed a little easier. After they had passed from their sight, he again motioned for them to stay still.

Finally, all clear. "Okay, I think we are ready to go."

"Who were they, Dad?" said Kyle.

"I don't know," said Dan, "but like us, they seem prepared for what is happening. Maybe they're living here in the woods. Maybe they are traveling somewhere. It doesn't matter, as long as they don't bother us."

Dan considered their chance encounter for a moment and wondered if the two men were on a trail. He motioned the family to follow him and they made a beeline for where the men had been walking. The path they found at the tree line was easier. A long walk later, the path took a decided turn north. Dan pulled out his GPS.

"Northeast now. River's right up ahead," he pointed.

He slipped the GPS back into his pocket and snapped it shut. They moved out, only to be slowed by thick sand pines, scratchy and sticky with sap. The grove seemed impossible until they heard the river ahead.

"Perfect," said Dan, "Lake Washington is just to the south."

"There is a lake here?" Cooper asked.

"Yeah, a swampy one. We can cross here and we are almost parallel with Melbourne. There is a spillway here, just a short walk east, but I don't think we can cross there."

Dan paused. All eyes were on him and he realized they were waiting.

"Let's check it out."

They walked another ten minutes and found where the water was forced up and over a barrier. A metal walkway topped both sandy banks. Nothing crossed. The river was wider, maybe twice as wide as earlier. And how much deeper?

"Maybe we're better off going back where the river isn't as wide," Dan said. "What do y'all think?"

Nobody answered. They knew he was thinking out loud and not really asking.

As they stood there, a pair of green drab Black Hawk helicopters roared overhead. They were just above the treetops and almost right on top of them. The thwump-thwump was immediate and deafening. Everyone dropped down lower, as if the machines were about to hit them. One banked slightly to turn and Dan looked at a machine gunner, sitting halfway out of the door. They were so close Dan could see the gunner speaking into his headset and the helicopters continued on.

"What are they doing here, Dad?" asked Kyle.

"Trying to restore order," said Dan, "and it's probably a good thing."

He continued. "Patrick Air Force Base is just a few miles from us. They're probably doing routine flyovers."

The group walked silently another five minutes, staying out of the grassy area immediately by the river. It was firm ground right down to the water. The river was about 30 yards across at this point and moving slow. Dan scanned for gators and snakes and saw nothing.

"Everybody undo the waist strap on your backpack. If you leave it on and you fall, you can drown," directed Dan. "I'll wade across first, see what the crossing is like and drop my gear on the other side. Then I will start back if all is okay. When I start back, you two boys come across. I'll bring Sophie and Mom."

Both boys nodded.

Dan loosened his backpack waist strap. He placed both rifles together and hoisted them up on his shoulder so that one hand swung free. He entered the water. Refreshing, about 60 degrees and dark, the tannin from cypress trees staining the water brown. Muck on the bottom, but his feet were not getting stuck. The water reached his waist then his chest. It didn't get much deeper.

By midstream, he felt a sense of relief. *This wasn't so bad,* he thought, *the kids should be able to do it.* Cooper will probably have to swim. *I can carry Sophie.* He lifted one foot and took the next step. His foot did not find the bottom this time. Dan disappeared.

Kate had been watching with a sense of dread when her confident husband slipped under. She yelled out to Dan when Cooper took her hand and motioned for her to be quiet.

12

TWO DOWN

Dan struggled underwater for a moment and then relaxed. It was nothing more than a drop off. He had gear, weapons and boots working against him. He let himself drift down for a few seconds until his feet touched bottom. Sand, he realized thankfully, and not muck. He bent his knees and pushed up, breaking the surface. A few seconds later, but they seemed like minutes. He kicked hard with his head up above the water.

"I'm okay," he called out, flashing the thumbs-up. He let himself drop again and realized it was only about eight feet deep. He kicked up again and tread water while moving forward. His feet brushed the bottom again and it was just a few seconds and he was on muck but able to stand up.

"Okay," he called again and pressed forward, just 20 feet from the water's edge. It was quickly getting shallow. He picked his legs up over the water and jogged just a little until he was up on the bank. He immediately dropped his pack and one of the rifles. He turned around to the other bank, ready to call out instructions.

His eyes narrowed.

The mystery man with the cowboy hat planted a foot in Kate's back and shoved her down to the sand. Even at this distance Dan heard her gasp as she hit the ground. The boys were laying flat. Sophie was nowhere in sight.

Dan swung the other rifle down onto his arm.

"Hey!" he yelled, "Knock it off!"

The man with the baseball cap carried his rifle slung back over his shoulder. He searched Kate's pack. Cowboy Hat turned and looked across the river.

"Shut the fuck up or we will do 'em," he yelled, his rifle pointed inches away from Kate's upper back.

A thousand thoughts flooded Dan's mind at once. His adrenaline immediately spiked and he could feel his focus sharpen. He dropped to the sand.

"Drop the fucking gun!" echoed from across the river.

Dan took up the shooter's position. His left leg was straight out behind him, his right leg was slightly bent. His waist and stomach pressed indentations into the dark river sand and his elbows and cheek were creating a three-point tripod for his AR-15.

"I said, drop the fucking gun!"

Dan had already made his decision. Months ago. He inhaled deeply and willed himself to relax. He had done this hundreds, if not thousands of times. His finger moved onto the trigger and he inhaled. Cowboy Hat was looking down at Kate and saying something and then looking back across the river at Dan.

"I'll kill her right after I fuck her if you don't put that gun down!"

Dan pursed his chapped lips. He shifted his sights to the left onto Baseball Cap. He was not even looking but was emptying the pack and checking each item. Dan could see him talking but could not make out the words. He paused on a first aid kit, tossing it over to a growing pile.

Dan moved his sights back onto Cowboy Hat. His finger pressure began to build. The gun jumped. A pink spray colored the air around Cowboy Hat's head. Dan was already refocusing. Baseball Cap turned toward his rifle. Dan squeezed again, slowly and with purpose. The gun bucked. Baseball Cap quickly twisted before he felt anything.

Cowboy Hat was just hitting the ground when Dan moved his sights back onto him.

KATE JUMPED. She grabbed Cowboy Hat's rifle and tried to shoot. It did not go off. She looked at it for a second. Dan knew she needed to rack a bullet with the bolt action. She tossed the rifle down and snatched the Glock from the pile. She turned and began emptying a magazine into Cowboy Hat. Dan was instinctively counting the shots in his head. She emptied the magazine.

"Kate!" Dan called but was ignored.

She searched her cargo pants pockets and pulled out another magazine. She shot at Baseball Cap. She stopped when the magazine was empty for a second time.

"Kate!" Dan could see her drop to her knees. Weeping. Kyle and Cooper stood up. Kyle scrambled over to squeeze his mom. He choked back an awful taste in his mouth.

Dan took the magazine out of his AR-15 and replaced the two spent bullets. He put the magazine in his pocket and left the rifle on the ground near the backpack. He picked up the other rifle he had discarded and waded back into the river with his pack.

By the time he had crossed over Sophie, Kyle and Cooper were surrounding Kate in a hug. Kate was sobbing uncontrollably and Dan joined in. Kate looked up at him and her face turned angry. She smacked him on the side of the head. "Don't you ever do that again."

Dan took the blow. "It's okay," he said. "Let it out. Let it all out."

She started crying again and Dan just held them all. After a minute, he stepped back.

He looked down and saw the bloodied remains of the two men. He shook his head and crouched on the ground looking away from the two evildoers. The adrenaline rush had been intense and now the aftermath was emotional. He was shaking. The wails of his wife was more than he could take. He began to weep. Soon they were all crying and Sophie was hugging Dan, her thin little arms wrapped around his neck.

"Where were you, Little Peep?" asked Dan.

"As soon as I saw them I ran into the brush," she said.

"That was smart," said Dan. "That was really smart of you."

"Dad, why would anybody want to hurt us?" she asked.

"I don't know, Little Peep," he said, "Try to take our gear, probably."

"No. They were going to kill us," Kyle said with conviction.

Dan swung his head around and flashed a father's look of anger at Kyle.

"Sorry," said Kyle. "But they were."

"I know," said Dan. "but let's not dwell on it. It happened. It's over. We gotta move on."

Dan stood and walked over to the two dead men's backpacks.

"Let's see what they have in their go bag," he said, unsnapping a clip.

On top he found a pair of night-vision goggles. He set them aside to keep. Some clothes, bottles of Deet, a compact hammock and a bag of toiletries. There was a serviceable water filter which he set aside to keep. A handgun and a box of ammo. He pulled it out to look at and decided it wasn't worth keeping because of the .308 bore size. He tossed the gun and ammo into the river. The wallet had some cash, which he pocketed.

"Hernando Negero," he read the Florida driver's license out loud.

The boys watched and Dan turned to the other bag. There was a mini Maglite which he gave to Cooper and a sharp hunting knife in a sheath. He handed that to Kyle. "Put that in your bag."

He then found a plastic baggie with what at first appeared to be credit cards. A couple were stuck together. As he separated them he realized it was dried blood. They were driver's licenses. Dan closed his eyes for a moment and took a deep breath. Had these men been killing people traversing the woods? It certainly looked like it. He put them back in the baggie. Nothing more of value.

Standing up, he reached for the rifles the men carried. The first was a surprise. It was a Mosin-Nagant, a Russian rifle manufactured by the millions and sold online dirt cheap. Dan remembered that these guns were numerous, cheap, and very accurate. He threw the weapon into the river. The other rifle was a semi-automatic Luger 9 mm. Dan decided to take it. He looked at the two bodies, wondering about ammo. One wore a waist pack. Dan extracted it and found a box of 9 mm and chewing tobacco. He handed the ammo to Kyle.

"Okay, let's get out of here."

Pointing toward the north, they walked in overwhelming sadness for about a minute and then sloshed into the river together. It was wider here, and the distance was further, but no deeper than about four feet. The only thing interesting was an alligator, too small to worry about. Upon exiting the river, they loaded up and started east toward the coast. Toward their warehouse. Toward safety?

Nobody said a word. The stress of the day settled deep into their psyche. The golden hue of the Florida sky at 3 pm added to the surreal feeling of impending doom that had descended on them.

13

JILLIAN

J illian Osborn waited in line at the ER. She had been sitting there for about three hours and she craved a cigarette. It wasn't likely that she was going to get one anytime soon, though. It did not appear that anybody was getting help at this emergency room. Jillian's mom needed oxygen. Over the past few months her breathing had grown more labored and now, with an almost empty tank, she and Jillian were desperate.

Usually, the health care assistant would call in an order. Two days later, a van delivered a new tank. The technician would bring it in, hook up the lines and check the flow. It was not always like that, but after her mother had made a mistake in changing tanks, the hospital had insisted on the full service. The oxygen shipment was now two days late. Calling the health company had yielded no answer and then a message that the voicemail was full. So, Jillian took matters into her own hands.

She had walked a long time from her mother's house to the hospital trailing a tank of oxygen on a small cart. She knew she would have to exchange the tanks and did not want to risk the walk twice. She did not know how far it was but she guessed it was over an hour-long walk. When she arrived at the medical center there was a long line.

It was finally her turn.

"My mom needs oxygen. I brought the tank to exchange it," said Jillian.

"Is your mother here?" the young woman asked in an unwelcoming tone.

"No, she ain't, she's in a wheelchair and can't walk, but I have all her paperwork and ID here," Jillian replied, reaching into her purse.

"Ma'am," the woman said quickly, "you can put it away. We are only handling life-threatening emergencies here. You do know that there is a state of emergency in Florida, right?

All over the country, for that matter." She dripped condescension.

"Yes," replied Jillian, "I know that, but my mother will probably die if she doesn't have oxygen."

They exchanged hostile stares. Finally, the receptionist said, "Let me see." She reached for the paperwork.

The receptionist scanned the first page and then began flipping through the pages, not really reading any of them.

"We don't stock oxygen but I can see if any can be delivered." She spun around in her chair and picked up a handheld radio.

"This is emergency intake," she said into the radio, "can we do an exchange on an oxygen cylinder for a lung cancer patient?" She let up on the button and sat motionless for a few seconds.

"Negative," the radio squawked, "the best we can do is maybe in a couple hours."

"Copy that." The receptionist swung toward Jillian. "Can you come back in two hours?"

Jillian inhaled and let it out in a sigh as she thought about the walk.

"I am just going to wait," she said, "it's a long walk home."

Now, three hours later, she was getting fidgety. In the time she had sat in the waiting room she had seen two men with gunshots come in, a couple of young men who were seriously injured from who knows what and now, a woman sat next to her with a bleeding forehead. And probably more people wearing masks than she'd ever seen. *It was the middle of the day*, she thought to herself, *where are all of these injuries coming from?* And she wasn't the only one waiting for oxygen. An elderly couple dragged a tank.

She was tempted to call Dog. It was a bad idea, and she knew it. She had to be home with her mother and Dog would beg her to come over to his place for sex or meet her at Red's bar.

And she would probably go. *Damn me!*

A feeling of loneliness stole over her but then she remembered her mother. She had a job to do and she was going to do it.

Jillian walked over to the receptionist.

"Excuse me," she said, "Can you check on the oxygen?"

"Sure," she replied, "give me a minute." She walked into the back office.

Jillian looked at her phone again. No signal. *That was strange*, she thought, *I'm almost downtown. Surely there must be a signal here.*

The receptionist returned.

"I am sorry, ma'am, but we don't have any oxygen and it doesn't look like any is on the way."

Jillian stared at her blankly for a moment. "So, what are we supposed to do, my mom will die without oxygen."

"I am sorry, ma'am. Check back tomorrow. Nothing is getting delivered today."

Jillian flashed anger. She held her composure and took a deep breath.

"Okay. Fine. Thanks."

She spun around, grabbed a hold of the handle of the cart with the empty oxygen tank and headed for the door. Still no phone signal. She stopped and swung back toward the receptionist.

"Does your phone work?"

"Yes, ma'am." Jillian turned back toward the reception desk. The receptionist held the phone's receiver out toward Jillian.

"Thanks."

Jillian read Dog's number as the receptionist punched it in. *Is he home or out drinking?*

The phone rang while Jillian bit her lip and waited.

"C'mon, Dog, pick up," she said under her breath.

On the fourth ring the phone was answered. She could hear him dropping the phone.

"Shit, sorry," he said, "yeah? Who is this?"

"Dog, it's Jillian. I need some help. I came here to the ER to get some oxygen for my mom but they didn't have any. I need to get home and I need to find some oxygen. Any ideas?"

"Well, hot damn, I just happen to have a car."

"Dog, are you drunk?"

"Nah." He had started drinking as soon as he could, but had fallen asleep. He had no idea how long he had slept but it couldn't have been more than an hour or two. "I had a couple but that was a while ago."

"Can you come get me?"

"You bet I can. Dog to the rescue. Tell me where again."

"South Regional, by 192. You know where that is, right?"

"Sure do," he said, "I am just over the causeway. Heading straight on over."

"Okay, Dog, thanks. This is important."

"I'll be there."

She checked the time and walked outside and sat down on a bench. She pined for a cigarette.

Dog looked around the kitchen and started opening up drawers. The keys were here somewhere. They had to be. He finished searching the kitchen and walked out into the living room. He spotted a side table. He opened the right hand drawer and found a black key fob.

As he turned around to leave he remembered the dead bodies. He paused to look outside left and right down the waterway. It was now early afternoon and he wondered who might be out and about. He went into the garage and looked around. The garage was impeccably clean and orderly, the domain of a Florida retiree with too much time on his hands. Hanging on one wall was a wheelbarrow, which he lifted down and walked it through the house and out the back patio. He went to a bedroom and grabbed some sheets. Dropping the sheets down on Ben's body, he lifted the man and marveled at how light he was in death. He carried him out to the wheelbarrow and pushed the shrouded body out to the dock. He stopped and dumped the body down on the dock, and then pushed it over underneath the railing. The water lapped up against the cement quay. A line of briny shells clung to the wall at the waterline. The splash was small and inconsequential considering it marked the end of a man's life.

He repeated the procedure with Claire's body and then he threw the wheelbarrow in the water on top of her. He could see Ben's body floating up to the surface shrouded in a light blue bedspread. He did not wait to see if Claire's body would surface. He stood up and rested his hands on the railing looking around casually. Nobody. He ran back to the house, grabbed a bottle of rum and lowered himself into the Lincoln. Where's the ignition? He finally realized that the car had a button to push and he laughed at himself. He pressed it and the car hummed. He revved it to make sure it was running. He started backing up and realized the gate was closed. On the visor he found a couple of remotes. He pressed the first one and the garage door started up. He pressed the other remote and the gate began to slide open.

"Holy shit," he out loud in pure admiration of rich people.

Putting the car in gear, he backed up onto the road and headed toward the causeway. The rum filled him with warm confidence as he thought about his mission. Jillian called *him* asking for help. *Dog to the rescue! Hot damn!*

14

GANOE

US Army Lieutenant James Ganoe sat in a metal folding chair with his arms folded across his chest. The room was quiet but full, with another dozen officers. Ten men and two women, Thomas noted, typical US Army distribution. A staff sergeant entered the room and he was followed by what appeared to be another officer. Thomas sat forward and tried to see the rank but there were no markings and no name tag on the uniform. *That was strange*, he thought.

The officer, if that is who he was, threw down a manila envelope and opened it up.

"My name is not important. I am just here to give you a briefing. I am from military intelligence."

"A spook," somebody behind him said. A few people chuckled. "I'm scared," the same voice said.

Somebody to Ganoe's left snickered but the spook had their attention and he looked up, scanning the room. After a dramatic pause he said, "Yeah, a spook. Something like that."

He paused again and then motioned for the staff sergeant to sit down if he wanted to, but the offer was declined. Instead, he backed up toward the door and faced the roomful of soldiers.

"This is a standard briefing, delivered across all contested areas," he began. Before he could continue, somewhere behind Thomas somebody asked, "What's a contested area?"

The presenter stopped and sighed deeply. *He was trying to think of the correct response,* thought Ganoe.

"A contested area is any place where freedom of movement may be in doubt," he replied. "There are about a dozen such places in Florida right now and many others across the country. Our job is to clamp people down and restore order, giving the food supply chain time to catch up and be delivered to the stores so nobody starves. It's as simple as that."

None of that info was new and had been delivered previously by his commanders. *Why this spook?* Ganoe wondered. As if on cue, he continued.

"I am here because we have decided to deploy drone assets into this corridor. There are citizens who are fearful and overreacting out of fear. That's mostly a police issue and we are not going to get involved. But, there are also armed militias forming in a few places and we intend to disarm and disperse them." The mood in the room changed again like rain clouds colliding. It was much more somber. Uniforms seemed to creak with too much starch. Chairs shifted and squeaked. Everybody knew that any action against militias meant shooting Americans.

"We will be coordinating with you over the next few days. I want you to understand the tactical position that we find ourselves in right now."

"Can we ask questions?" came the same voice from behind Ganoe.

The presenter stopped again and was obviously annoyed.

"Sure," he said, "you can ask questions."

"Are we going to be shooting civilians?"

The joking was over.

"Martial law has been declared and we will enforce it," he said tersely.

"What is the situation nationally?" Again, it was the voice from behind him and Ganoe slowly turned in this chair to see who it was. It was an officer he had never met.

"Most of the contested areas are in urban centers. The local police have done their best, but the National Guard has been deployed in all 50 states."

"We ain't National Guard," somebody else interrupted.

"Yeah, you, the US Army, are in charge of a lot of things that they can't handle."

"Like shooting Goddammned Americans?"

The spook stared back at the joker-turned-accuser. He let the question hang in the air.

"If you aren't ready to protect the United States against all enemies, foreign and domestic, then you should have a talk with your CO."

Silence again.

"We'll be keeping up food stocks, ensuring water and electricity are not disrupted *and* addressing any armed insurrection. We have decided to prioritize high traffic areas where shipments of food and other supplies come in. I-95 here is one such route we intend to keep open."

"Why?" This time the voice was from Ganoe's right and he looked down to see a female lieutenant. She paused and then continued, "Why are we at this readiness state when there isn't an identified enemy?"

"There is an enemy, ma'am, and it is called fear. Any city in America is about 72 hours away from having no food. Just-in-time inventory systems make sure that stores are not stocked," he said.

"How many police are there in proportion to civilians?" she asked.

"I'll tell you. Nationally, there are about 3.4 civilian and sworn police officers for every 1,000 people. How many are needed to keep order as people run out of food, water and electricity? A helluva lot more than that, I can assure you."

Before he could stop himself Ganoe asked, "How long is this expected to go on?"

The presenter responded immediately, "We don't know. The

nukes used in Southeast Asia will create a climatic disturbance. The last one was substantially larger than the tactical nukes used in the first days of the conflict. You know that a large fire burns across large portions of India and southern Pakistan. The initial series of bomb created a zone of heat so hot that it vaporized a city of some 11 million people. The Pakistani response resulted in 4 more cities being hit inside India. All big cities, all burning uncontrolled at this point. The nuclear fallout is their problem. Our problem is rapid climate change and a failing ecosystem."

There was more to say, but everybody in the room knew that it would not be said.

He continued, "You can see that with your own eyes every time you step outside. Chances are pretty good that this will last a long time but we don't know. Our first challenge is to make sure that our public support systems continue to operate."

"How much of a food supply is there?"

The presenters shrugged, "There are estimates, of course. But nobody really knows. If there is a drop in temperature, this will affect us for years to come. But, there may be time to adjust our crop strategy. The biggest and perhaps most difficult phase will be in the next few weeks. If we manage to maintain a sense of civil life, we can probably go a lot longer."

"Looks like we fixed global warming!" said the soldier sitting next to Ganoe. He looked around with a smile but nobody was laughing.

Over the next half hour the group learned about the capabilities that were available to them, what sort of force protection rules were to be in place and the rules of engagement. The briefing reminded Ganoe of his time in Iraq. He had arrived years after the main fighting and was mostly in charge of guarding the Green Zone around Baghdad. This time around, it would be on American streets with American citizens in the mix. He could not imagine that anybody would be stupid enough to take on the US Army.

"Finally, there is an important issue we will be addressing with urgency," the military intelligence officer said. "We are aware of armed patrols in the area known as Deseret Ranch. There is some sort of militia effort being organized. We'll be watching this area and we will meet force with force if necessary."

Ganoe shook his head. Could he do it? Would he pull the trigger if the target was an American?

15

I-95

I-95 rose up over the brush as they walked forward. It was now late afternoon and the sun was sinking behind them creating a spectacular golden sunset. Dan saw a column of black smoke rising on the horizon to the south. He looked more carefully and realized that there were a number of different smoking columns rising up over south Melbourne, toward Patrick Air Force Base.

"There's a curfew," he said. "We don't want to be on the streets at sunset. Let's camp out here one more night and cross over in the morning."

Backpacks immediately hit the ground.

"Hang on, guys, this isn't a good spot for us," said Dan, "Kyle and Cooper, why don't y'all scout a place for us?"

The two boys were eager, Kyle leading the way. Sophie walked over to Dan and put her head against him and hugged his thigh.

"We are taking a break, tonight, Little Peep," said Dan, running his hand through her hair.

A weary, bleary eyed Kate looked on. She had not spoken for two hours.

"We should be to the warehouse tomorrow, Kate," Dan said. She stared at him blankly and then looked away.

"You'll feel better after a good sleep," he said.

"Will I?"

Dan stayed silent. After a few moments he said, "This is tough stuff, I know that."

"My 14-year-old killed a man yesterday and today my husband killed two," she replied with a flat, monotone voice. "Yeah, I'd say it's tough stuff."

"Those men were all going to harm us. Or worse. Babe, we had no choice."

"You always have a choice."

"Yeah, on second thought you are right. We made our choice and we aren't going to back off. We are going to survive this."

"And then what?" she asked. "Our kids will be killers."

Dan cradled Sophie's blond head in his hand and continued to stroke her hair. He took a deep breath. "Listen, this is all happening fast. It's probably going to get worse before it gets better. If we can get out to sea and stay out of harm's way, maybe the government will reassert itself and we can come back. For now, we need to protect ourselves and get to the boat."

"I am not sure it's worth it."

"Kate, hang with me. We'll work hard to keep our faith, our family and our future. We must do the things that keep us human, even now."

"All I know is that in the last 48 hours I have seen murder committed by my own child and husband. Now you're making it about faith and family."

"That's not fair and you know it. Cooper did the right thing. Those men were not going to take our truck. They were going to take everything and leave us for dead. Those two bad asses today had a stack of IDs in their backpack. They've been out killing already. We got lucky."

Just then Kyle came out of the brush, rifle shouldered.

"Found a great place," he said, "among some oak and palm trees not five minutes from here."

Kyle looked at his mom and then his dad, a knowing look coming across his face.

"Do you need some time to talk?"

"No," said Kate, "We don't. Let's go."

Kyle led them back to Cooper, who had gathered a pile of firewood and was sitting on a piece of corrugated sheet metal.

"Coop," said Dan, "did you look under that tin before you sat on it?"

Cooper stood up slowly, nodding no. He stepped off gingerly as Dan poked a stick under the tin and slowly lifted it. A long black snake sat coiled.

"Aw, it's just a black racer," said Cooper. He used his boot to trap the snake against the ground and then picked it up, pinching it behind the neck.

"Next time it might be something worse," said Dan. "Be more careful."

Cooper nodded.

Soon, all the hammocks were slung and the family circled around a small cook stove heating up water.

"Mac and cheese," said Kyle, "my specialty." Soon, they were eating a gooey, half-cooked few ounces of carbohydrates from mess kits. All but Kate, who ate nothing, sitting in silence.

A vehicle broke the silence. "That's a reassuring sound," he said. "Maybe the roads are open."

They cleaned up as it was getting darker. The haze overhead and the trees made seeing the point of sunset impossible, but it was obviously about time.

"Kyle," said Dan, "Take a rifle and stand watch for a few minutes. Cooper and I can scout out the highway."

"No," said Kate. "You left us today and look what happened."

"I am sorry, it's necessary. Kyle is here and will be on watch, right, Kyle?"

"Yes sir," said Kyle.

"Grab your radio, Kyle, put it on channel 5 and hold it in one hand. Key it down twice if there is any problem." He adjusted the squelch on his radio and connected an earbud. He grabbed the night-vision goggles pulled them on his head and powered them on.

He stood up and walked over to Kate, picked her rifle up and handed it to her. "You are on watch, too," he said. "Between the two of you, nothing should be able to approach without you knowing it."

She looked at him with a pout.

"Sorry, this is what we've been dealt." He leaned into her and whispered, "Be on the team."

Her eyes welled up with tears. "I am sorry, I am so sorry." The rifle began to slide from her hands as she began to weep.

Dan bearhugged her and pulled her head into his shoulder. "It's okay," he said. "It's a lot to take in." Sophie walked up and wrapped her arms around them both and Kate chuckled through her tears.

She looked up at him. "I am okay. You go and do what you have to do."

"We'll be quick," he said. "Let's go, Coop."

They covered the distance back toward their original spot in less than ten minutes. As they got closer to the highway the sound of engines and tires grew. It was not quite right, though. More sound than there should be.

The GPS told him homes were a quarter-mile away. All dark. I-95 black with no street lights. He could see the strip where the highway lay. They advanced another hundred yards to see a moving snake. A snake more like a train.

He flipped down his night-vision goggles and hit the button to turn them on. They flashed on for a second and then immediately turned themselves off. They were meant for full darkness and had a light shut-off if conditions were too bright. Dan fumbled with an adjustment ring to no avail. He found another ring and slowly twisted it. The display, a round reticule, began to turn dark green. An image appeared but it was out of focus. He turned the other ring and the highway abutment snapped into view. Behind it was the train he had seen. Humvees, armored personnel carriers and light armored vehicles. He looked left and he looked right. It was nothing but drab green and camouflaged military vehicles as far as he could see in both directions.

16

OXYGEN

The best thing about this car was the power, thought Dog as he accelerated over the causeway. He punched the radio. It was somebody talking about a state of emergency. He hit the second button and found the same broadcast. On the third button he got a Spanish voice. He turned off the radio. A few seconds later, he turned it on again and pressed the CD button. Jazz music floated over the speakers. He turned it off again.

He rolled down the window to be greeted by a tornado of salty air tinged with smoke. He was the only car on the causeway and he was doing about 75. He started the drop back down toward the city from the highest point on the bridge. A sight he did not expect.

Black, smoky columns rising up from Melbourne to the left and right. The sky was auburn and the sun held the color of sunset yet it was midday. A few street lights were on. No pedestrians. There were few cars out, save a couple ahead of him about a quarter-mile. They were moving slow and he realized he was quickly catching up to them. He instinctively braked.

Tail lights of the leading car flickered for a second, and then the car appeared to accelerate. It was hard for him to see from this distance and angle. Then a barricade in the road. He slowed further.

The car ahead was trying to smash through. Dog stopped in the middle of the road.

The next car in line was copying the first, accelerating toward the barrels. Dog realized that there were people standing on both sides of the bridge and they were rolling out orange barricade barrels to slow down the traffic. Dog smiled. *These were his people,* he thought, *better than coming up on the cops.* He snatched the handgun and pulled back the rack. A bullet in place. He knew what he had in the magazine. Gun in his left hand, floating out the window, he hit the gas.

The car spun out and for a second Dog almost lost control. He did not expect that the Town Car would have this much power. *All the better.* He was now closing in on car number two and risked a rear-end collision. He aimed the handgun forward and pulled back on the trigger. A loud shot echoed in the car. The crowd dropped down to the ground. He braked right behind the other car. As he got closer, he could see heads peeking above the barrels. He squeezed another wild shot and the heads went down. Dog leaned forward, and stuck his arm out in front of the windshield and got off another round. He drove cleanly through the intersection and slowed again, aiming somewhere behind him. He shot again and did not even look back at the chaos he just stoked.

He aimed straight west for a few blocks until he came to Dixie Highway and then turned south. Within a few minutes he was at the ER. Jillian was sitting out front, on a bench. She had an oxygen tank cart parked next to her. Dog pulled up in front of her.

"You all good?" he asked.

Her face betrayed tears. She opened her mouth to talk and then stopped, tears brimming on her eyelids.

"What's wrong, Jill?" Dog asked, gently cupping her chin and pulling her face up to him. She turned away and said nothing.

"Jill, I'm here. What's wrong?"

She was silent and he held her face in his filthy hands. He wondered if he had done something and let her go. Dog sat down on the bench next to her. She tried to talk and resumed crying. She buried her head in his chest and he cradled her. He began thinking through the last hour for mistakes he might have made. He couldn't come up with anything. He was quiet and just held her. After a few minutes her crying subsided.

"Dog," she said, "I need oxygen for Mom. I can't go back without it. She might not make it through the night."

"They didn't have any here?"

"They have it, I think, but they don't have any for us. I don't know for sure, but I think they have it." Her eyes flooded again.

"Hang on," he said, "let me talk to them." Dog got up. "Get in the car," he said, "I'll be back."

The big glass doors were no longer sliding open so Dog pushed through the side door. He approached the main desk and, placing his forearms on the counter, leaned over, ignoring the man currently talking with the receptionist.

"I need some oxygen or somebody is going to die," he said loudly and flatly.

The receptionist flashed an irritated look and slid her eyes over to Dog for just one second. "Wait your turn." She then continued her conversation.

Dog inhaled loudly. Years of being in institutions had taught him to be subservient to receptionists. They often held the keys to whatever kingdom they ruled. Dog tapped his thumbs on the counter top lightly while looking down at his hands. The conversation droned on.

Finally, after sixty seconds but what felt to Dog like sixty minutes, the conversation drew to a close. Dog was staring at the receptionist.

He leaned over and repeated, "I need a tank of oxygen or somebody is going to die."

A thin Hispanic woman stepped up into the place where the previous man had stood. She was clutching a transparent file folder and began extracting a prescription from it.

"Sir," the unhappy receptionist said, "you need to wait your turn." She pointed to the line that Dog just spotted. Dog realized that the entire room was one snaking line of people, mostly sitting down. His anger flashed and the gun in his pocket gained ten pounds of weight as he pondered the new reality.

"This isn't going to work," he said flatly. "Who's in charge?"

"I am," said the receptionist, her flat voice sharpening and her no-nonsense stare telling Dog he had kicked the hornet's nest. "And you can step back in line."

"The fuck I can," he replied reaching into his right pocket and finding the assuring grip of the gun. He whipped the weapon out in his right hand resting it on the counter top casually.

The receptionist reached under her desk.

"Don't," said Dog sliding the weapon over so that the barrel pointed at her. She froze.

"Pick up the phone and ask for some oxygen," he commanded. "And no shit from you. I only want to hear about the oxygen."

The old man standing next to him froze. He turned toward Dog slowly. Dog, without warning, hit him in the mouth with the pistol before he could utter a word

"Shut the hell up," he said. The man stumbled back a step and brought his hands to face, blood immediately streaming through his fingers. Dog had spliced his lip.

"Get it now and no shit from you," said Dog, turning back to the woman.

"Yes sir." She picked up the phone and punched a button.

"I need an oxygen canister right away," she said. There was a pause, "I know, I need an oxygen canister right away." Another pause ensued, "I don't know," she replied. "Just bring one out."

"The kind that fits on a cart," Dog said.

She nodded and then said, "For a mobile cart, please, and hurry."

She looked at Dog with angry eyes. "It's coming."

Dog stepped to the right and reached over, grabbing the old man who had taken a step back and was holding his hands over his mouth. Dog grabbed his arm and pulled him close. Closer than six inches. He pushed the barrel of the gun into his side.

"No shit now," he said flatly.

The doors behind the reception desk swung open and a young man in hospital scrubs was lugging an oxygen tank in one hand and walking with a swagger. He stopped immediately and looked first at Dog, then the hostage.

"Keep coming," said Dog.

The man with the tank stood still. He looked down at the reception. She nodded to indicate that he should continue. He brought the tank around the edge of the reception desk and set it down. He raised his hands slightly and backed off, eyeballing Dog the whole time.

Dog held onto the old man's bony arm and kept the gun in place. He pulled him in close and walked sideways to the left toward the tank.

"Grab it," said Dog.

The man lifted the top of the tank and Dog backtracked toward the door. The tank scraped across the floor as Dog pulled both of them along. When they reached the side door, Dog let go of the man's arm and reached for the tank. The old man's thin, weathered hand was still clutching the top of the tank. He didn't let go as Dog's hand tried to grasp the metal connector and black knob.

"This is wrong," the old man said.

Dog looked him in the eye and pursed his lips. Dog's head slowly moved back and then came forward in a flash. Dog's forehead connected with the man's nose with a beefy thud. He dropped to the floor lifeless.

Dog looked up at the silent room, all eyes on him. He lifted the pistol up and pointed to the closest person in the room. A young girl clutching a phone stared with wide eyes.

"Nobody fucking moves. I will be right back."

Dog pushed through the door. Jillian's head was buried in her hands in the passenger seat. Dog tossed the tank into the backseat, shut the door and yanked open his door.

"Got it." He smiled at Jillian as he dropped the car into gear.

"That was so quick," she said as he punched the gas, "how did you do it?"

"I just asked," he said, "They have plenty of tanks. You just have to tell them you really need it."

She pushed up the armrest in the middle of the seat and slid over to his side, just like high school. She laid her head down on his shoulder. "Thank you, thank you so much."

Heading toward Jillian's mother's house, they careened down the street, a police car approaching in the opposite direction at high speed. They passed and Dog looked in the rearview mirror. The cruiser turned into the hospital parking lot.

17

HUMAN

The family huddled in a circle back at camp, the smell of bug spray thick in the air.

"We are going to clear out right before sunrise and try for the warehouse. Maybe about four hours using back roads," said Dan, his GPS in his hand. "We hope we come up in a neighborhood where we'll blend in."

"Why are all the military vehicles out?" asked Kate.

"Well, Patrick Air Force Base is just south a few miles. They may be staging from there. They could fly all of those vehicles in on C-130s," said Dan.

He pulled out the shortwave radio and tuned it to the AM band. He fiddled until a voice was audible. It was repeating the emergency declaration. Dan shut it off.

"Let's set up camp out of sight, back from the road a good ways," he said.

They silently went about their work, each setting up their own hammock. Kyle helped Sophie and Dan set up the camp stoves. They were soon eating ramen and sipping orange drink mixed from powder. They were tired and nobody was in a mood to talk.

As they finished, Dan spoke. "In the morning, we will wrap our rifles in the hammocks. No need to advertise that we are armed. Might keep attention off of us."

"Dad, why don't we just walk in the dark tonight?" asked Cooper.

"The curfew would be a bigger problem for us than anybody we might meet along the way tomorrow," he said. "They are moving soldiers and military police into populated areas where we're headed. For all we know, there are checkpoints and they won't be forgiving."

Dan stood awkwardly. Pockets sewn into the inside of his pants were filled with gold coins. Their heaviness was chafing his waist. There was a deep soreness in his chest from the backpack straps. "We are close, guys, we just need to press on a little further. Let's get some sleep and make the final push in the morning."

Kate looked up. He looked down and saw her eyes, gaunt and defeated. Her jawline set hard and her natural beauty gone in somber sadness. He had a moment of doubt and wondered if they made a mistake leaving their home. He knew that was Kate's unspoken view. She had seen her little boy and husband kill strangers. She had put up with Dan's constant worry about the future and preparations for anarchy. Now that future was here.

He had moved from one world to another without questioning. She was stuck in last week, a job, cars, a house and kids' programs. He knew that he led his family to safety but his little army was not with him one hundred percent. A flash of emotion swept over him. He faltered.

"Dad." It was Cooper. "You okay?"

"Yeah," he replied with a husky voice, "just a bit overwhelmed for a moment. Let's clean up and get to sleep."

"We can't ever go back, can we?" asked Kate.

"We don't know that, babe," Dan replied, "most people think that after society has a breakdown like this, order will return after a short time. It might be that we are already past the worst of it, or it might go on for a while. We just don't know."

"We killed people," she said flatly.

"We did that in self-defense, Kate. We're not like them. We are not taking what belongs to others or threatening anybody to get what we want. But we have a right to defend ourselves," he said.

"What about turn-the-other-cheek?"

"Kate, if you and I were alone, if we only had ourselves to worry about, then we could do that. But we aren't alone. We have a family and a duty to protect each of these kids and that means protecting ourselves as well. We are their best bet."

The three kids sat stone still, listening.

"I have spent most of my adult life healing people, and now we're killers," she said. "I don't feel like we are even human anymore."

"Kate, we've talked about this before. We have chosen survival over being victims. I am not standing by while a couple of renegades hurt my family. I feel no guilt about what happened, for me or for Cooper."

Kate dropped her head in her hands and began to weep. Dan dropped down on one knee behind her and rubbed her back, drawing her close for a hug. She pushed him away.

"Promise me that we won't become like them," she said between sobs, "Promise me that we won't use our own survival as an excuse to hurt others."

"Kate, I promise we will do whatever we can to be good people. We'll help others when we can. But we need to protect each other first."

"I want to pray," said Kate.

"Okay," said Dan, "let's pray. Come here." Dan waved the kids over. They huddled together with arms wrapped around each other.

"Heavenly Father," and he led them in a prayer as Kate and Sophie cried. Kyle and Cooper didn't close their eyes but looked on blankly.

18

CIVILIZATION

Dan was up around 3 am. He silently unzipped his hammock and dropped down to the ground; he slept in his boots. He planned a one-hour walk to determine their best route forward. He walked over to Kyle's hammock and unzipped it, reaching in and waking the sleeping teenager.

Kyle bolted straight up. He looked at his dad with wide eyes as Dan held a finger over his lips. He motioned for Kyle to get down.

"Get your rifle and stand guard," whispered Dan, "and let's coordinate our radios."

Dan had taught the boys the radio frequency shifts based on 15 minute intervals. Kyle nodded as he slipped on his boots and walked to the edge of the undergrowth.

"No sitting down," his dad said, barely audible. "It'll be too easy to fall asleep. Set the radio squelch high so there is no hiss."

Kyle nodded when he was ready.

"One hour," said his father, "Be back then."

Dan hustled out into the darkness toward the interstate. After retracing their earlier route he came within sight of I-95. The moving snake of vehicles was nowhere in sight. The huge sodium-vapor bulbs that typically shed an orange light on the roadway were all dark. Save for the low-hanging moon it would have been ink black. There was no early dusk glow from the west.

Dan angled south until he came to a fence. He walked along it to the south until he came to an intersection which he identified as the dead end of 404. He studied his GPS; this was an excellent place to cross. To the north was a subdivision, but here they could easily get across I-95 and then walk through any number of residential streets and backyards. He marked the GPS waypoint and took one long, last look. Movement on the road. He dropped his pack and fished out the night-vision goggles. A Humvee sat parked, a gun turret set high and a gunner moving back and forth with the weapon. He was smoking a cigarette.

Why station a sentry here? There were few people at this intersection. It must be, he concluded, a means of keeping drivers from either entering or exiting I-95. Perhaps it was to protect the convoy. In any case, there would be no crossing here unless the situation changed.

Dan checked his watch, he was only 15 minutes out from camp. He'd wait and watch.

After about ten minutes, the driver emerged from the Humvee. The two soldiers spoke but Dan could hear nothing. The driver interrupted the conversation and quickly returned to the cab. Dan thought it must be a radio transmission. The Humvee started up and circled around to head under the 404. Shortly thereafter, Dan saw the headlights wash across the freeway as the armored vehicle evidently turned north.

Dan keyed his radio down. He whispered "Back in fifteen. Is all okay?"

"Yes sir, all good."

Back at camp, he told Kyle he could go back to bed. Dan sat up and pulled out the GPS unit and began looking at the streets, the distances, the best routes and where they might hole up if needed. He had one phone hidden away and was tempted to turn it on to check local news reports but thought better of it. He could be tracked. He sat down with his back against a palm tree, using his backpack for a cushion. His rifle between his legs, he felt prepared but very tired.

He awoke with a start. The sun was up and had just cleared the trees to cast a warm glow. He was sweating. How had he fallen asleep, he wondered? He looked at his watch and was amazed to see that it was almost 7:45. He was angry with himself. He had wanted to cross over just as soon as the curfew was lifted. The sky was about as clear as Dan had seen it in weeks.

"Hey, let's get a move on," he said. He gave Sophie's hammock a small shove.

"Good morning, Daddy," she said.

"C'mon Coop, c'mon, Kyle, rise and shine," Kate's hammock zipper opened and she began to turn.

"What time is it?" she asked.

"Almost 8," he said, "I let you sleep in."

"Why do I feel so tired, then?" she asked. She stood and rubbed her back. "I hate that thing."

"Hopefully, we'll reach the warehouse tonight," said Dan.

The boys were packing up their gear. Dan stopped them, saying "Let's wrap the rifles up in the hammocks."

Dan lit the stove and put a pot of water on to boil.

"Can I have some coffee, Daddy?" Sophie asked.

"Sure, get your gear packed up and you can have a cup." They were all growing up fast now. The thought of his little girl drinking coffee made him smile.

Soon, they were eating packets of steaming oatmeal. Dan, Kate and Sophie had cups of coffee and the boys were drinking powdered orange juice. They finished, cleaned up, put on their packs and picked up their wrapped rifles. Stepping out onto Dan's trail, they marched toward the 404.

As they neared the road, Dan stopped and turned to the family.

"Stay here, I'll check things out," he said.

He walked ahead of them and came to the dead end road. There was a chain link fence but a large swath of it had been pulled down, as if somebody had successfully driven over it. Nobody was in sight. Dan waved the family forward.

They scrambled over the fence and walked forward about 150 feet and found themselves on the overpass, above I-95. It was quiet and they had a good view of the surrounding area. Dan looked left and right. As far as the road snaked out it was empty.

They continued west and came down to street level. Dan knew that there was a neighborhood off to the south. They soon began to see the backs of houses. He contemplated cutting through the houses to get off of 404. Not quite a mile ahead lay the main entrance to the development and he decided to wait until they reached it.

The whoop-whoop of a helicopter drew close. It was soon above them and then jerked in a wide arc. A soldier in camo was sitting behind a large gun, the doors of the helicopter open. It took a lazy spiral closer to them. The gunner sighted them in. Dan felt the punch of adrenaline.

"Dad, what are they doing?" whispered Kyle.

"I don't know," Dan replied. His mind skipped to the man shot on the road and the two by the river. Could the chopper crew be looking for them? His pulse was quickening.

A Humvee pulled out from the residential road ahead, driving directly toward them.

19

SERGEANT PEARCY

The Humvee rolled up to them, one gunner with a machine gun sitting up on the turret. Metal plates lined the turret and a soldier, likely a reservist, sat low in his seat.

A loudspeaker boomed, startling them all.

Sophie started crying.

"Are you armed?"

Dan was not sure of himself. "Uh, yeah, sort of."

"Place everything on the ground and back up a few steps."

Dan looked at Kate and the kids, nodding to comply. He stooped down and set the two guns on the pavement. The others did the same. They instinctively began to show their open palms and they stepped back. Dan remembered the gun in his waistband, offset to the right but under his shirt. He didn't say anything about it, though. Reaching for it might indicate hostile intentions.

The passenger door of the Humvee opened up and a small, thin soldier stepped out.

"Do you have ID?"

"Yes, of course. I am going to drop this pack down and take it out, okay?" said Dan.

"Nice and easy, please."

"Is there a problem here? Did we do something to warrant this stop?"

"Where are you coming from?"

"The swamp. We walked here from over by Orlando," said Dan.

"We drove part of the way," said Kyle.

Dan shot him a look that said, "Shut up!"

"We left our car on the other side of the swamp and have been walking for a couple days," Dan filled in.

"There is martial law on, you know," said the soldier.

"Only until 6 am, though, right?"

"You can't be on the streets until 6, but it's martial law 24/7."

The gunner in the turret spoke up, "It's damn dangerous out here. You are going to get those kids killed."

Dan handed over his license. "What's the chance you can drop us off on the other side of town?"

His question was ignored as the soldier backed up and passed the license through the open door to somebody inside. Likely an officer.

"We are going to run your license and if it comes back clean, you can go on," he said. "You are going to leave the weapons, though."

"Hell I am," said Dan, "you can't do that."

The soldier shot him an icy stare. Dan held his gaze and the soldier said, "We are here because yesterday, two soldiers were shot and killed on the 404, about a quarter mile from here. We are under orders to take any weapons we see."

Dan said nothing.

A voice from inside the truck said, "Monroe, here you go, let 'em go."

As Monroe turned to take back the license there was a thud. He stepped sideways as if he were shoved. He looked down at his side and then wiped his hand across his lower stomach. He held his bloody hand up to his face.

"Shooter!" came from the turret. Monroe went down on one knee. Kate stepped forward and the turret spun around on her, the large caliber weapon focused on her. "Get back!" screamed the gunner. The Apache helicopter reappeared, low and over the houses. The radio chattered inside the Humvee.

Kate put her hands up higher and lowered her head but kept moving forward.

"I am a physician's assistant," she said, "I can help him."

Monroe crumbled onto the pavement.

Dan spun in a circle and commanded, "Everybody get low. Go around the back of the vehicle. The shot came from that way." The gunner disappeared into the Humvee and the passenger door slammed.

Dan looked at the windshield of the Humvee and pointed his finger shouting, "You stay there, you stay there!"

The kids scrambled around the backside of the big, tan armored vehicle. Dan dragged the injured private around the backside of the vehicle. A heavy gun thudded in the background somewhere.

Kate knelt down over Monroe as Dan pulled a knife from under his pant leg. He cut back the uniform and ripped it all the way open. Kate motioned to Dan to grab her backpack. He sprinted out in front of the Humvee and came back around, already ripping open the top.

Kate had rolled the young man gently forward and was feeling his back for an exit wound.

"Nothing back here," she said. She pulled off her shirt and wadded it up, briefly rubbing the wounded area and then she pushed down on the wound.

"Make sure his airway is clear," she commanded. Dan said, "It's all good, he is breathing."

Monroe's eyes were wide and he stared up. "Am I dying?" he asked, "Am I dying? Hell, it hurts so bad."

"No, no, you are going to be fine," replied Kate, "Dan, press down here, hard. Really hard."

He leaned over the wounded soldier, pressing down with both hands, his arms straight.

Kate searched her pack and then said, "I am going to give you something for the pain. Tell me, how old are you?"

"Nineteen," Monroe replied.

"Where you from?"

"Alabama," he said, "Birmingham, Alabama."

"Are you a 'Bama football fan?" She pulled out a sealed packet with a needle and a small vial.

"Yes, ma'am," he said, "I sure am."

"You are in trouble, then," said Kate, "because I am a Florida State fan."

Monroe chuckled through his tears. "Well, I am sorry about that ma'am, not much I can do about it."

Kate smiled as she poked the small vial with the needle, drew the plunger back, and filled the tube.

"This is going to make you feel better in just a moment," she said. "Kyle, tell the men in the Humvee that we need him moved to a hospital."

Kyle stood and the window rolled down an inch before he could.

"Helicopter is on its way," came a voice, and then the window rolled back up.

Dan looked up. A house bordering the 404 burned, about five or six homes down from where they stood. A helicopter was still poised above, as if suspended from the black clouds.

"Ma'am," asked Monroe, "how bad is it?"

"The bullet didn't come through your back," she said, "which is good."

Kate placed the vial in his hand.

"When the helicopter comes, you give this vial to the doctor so he knows I gave this to you."

"I feel better already, ma'am, thanks."

A second helicopter, smaller but incredibly loud, appeared from over the houses. It circled once and began to descend onto the blacktop.

Dan yelled to the Humvee, "Hey, did you get the shooter?"

There was no response.

The second Bell medevac helicopter set down, the door slid open and a couple of medics rushed out with a stretcher.

Kate advised them: "One bullet entered in the lower abdomen and he was bleeding pretty profusely. It might have struck the iliac artery. He needs lots of pressure until you can stanch that bleeding."

She took Monroe's hand and pulled the vial from it.

"I gave him this. He is in shock and I would bet his blood pressure is dangerously low."

"We know what to do, ma'am," said one of the medics. He began prepping the stretcher while the other medic dropped to the casualty's side and grabbed his arm. In short order he had inserted an IV needle and was connecting a bottle of saline.

"When we transfer him to the cot," said the other medic to Dan, "try to keep pressure on."

Another Humvee, with no gun turret, had arrived. Dan had not heard it or seen it drive up. An officer was addressing the two soldiers sitting in the first vehicle.

"Okay, let's get ready," said a medic. They had grabbed Monroe's shoulders and feet. "We are going to roll him this way, shove the stretcher up under him and then slide him the other way."

Dan complied and kept the pressure on. The stretcher was now under Monroe and Dan was still kneeling over him.

"Okay, let's lift him, keep the pressure on, don't worry about us, we can lift him with the pressure."

Dan rose and they walked toward the helicopter. Setting the stretcher inside, one medic leapt inside, motioned Dan off and immediately took over, leaning hard on the wound. The other medic was putting a cuff on the arm.

"Thank you, sir," said Monroe, "and tell the doc thanks." Dan could barely hear him above the engine and rotor noise.

"I will," yelled Dan.

"Hey," screamed the medic leaning over the wounded soldier, "you saved his life. Good job."

Dan nodded. As he turned around, he saw Kate walking toward the colonel. Behind her, more vehicles turned the corner, heading toward them. Kate stopped in front of the officer. She put one hand on her hip and stuck her other index finger in his face. An Apache attack helicopter circled overhead. Dan could barely hear her, but she was shouting. The only words he heard were, "You put us at risk!"

He smiled inwardly. She was a survivor.

20

MOM

Dog got a hero's treatment, arriving back at the trailer house where Jillian had been caring for her mom. Jillian had fawned over him and when she told the old lady how he had saved the day, her eyes flooded with tears of joy. *Damn*, thought Dog, *I did real good.*

Jillian cooked a light meal and to Dog's utter amazement, he was invited to stay the night. The old lady had always considered Dog the worst person in Jillian's life. She had done everything a mom could do, short of disowning her own daughter, to keep her from Dog.

When they had hooked up the tank and gotten the oxygen flowing again, the old lady had come alive in a way he had never seen. She had ordered Jillian to bring out a bottle of Gentleman Jack and poured him a huge tumbler. He had never tasted anything so smooth and full of fire before. They relaxed and laughed together. Dog marveled at the turnaround.

Jillian had cooked up some pasta and spread a jar of sauce over it all, joking about her Italian heritage. They sat and ate while watching television. News on every channel headlined the bank shortages, the gas shortages, shootings, and just when the president was about to address the nation, the power failed. *Sweet relief*, thought Dog.

I don't want to be on the damn news. He thought about going out but changed his mind when Jillian ran her hand across his crotch.

By 7 the old lady was in bed. Jillian sat with Dog on the couch. They lit a few candles.

"So romantic," Jillian said, "don't you think?"

"Yeah," he said, "I guess."

"Where'd you get the car?"

"Just a friend," he said. "Figured he wouldn't be needing it with all the troubles."

She looked at him knowingly. He knew she knew. But she didn't press it. They were soon deep into a session of lovemaking, right there on the living room. He felt like a high school boy.

After they were finished, Jillian shoved him down on the couch and told him to stay put. She went into the bathroom while he fished out a cigarette.

"You can't smoke in here," she said when she returned mostly naked. "It really bothers Mom."

He looked at her but kept smoking. The mood shifted.

"Can you step out back and finish that?" she asked, "C'mon, I'll go with you."

She was wearing panties and had a blanket wrapped around her top. They stood and walked out the back door of the trailer. There was loud, thumping rap music coming from a trailer just down the street. Flickering candles casting a funny light from a few windows and an acrid smell filled the air.

"What do you think is going on?"

"I don't know," he said, "some rag heads started a nuclear war somewhere and the whole system is fucked up."

"Will this last long?"

"How the hell would I know?" He instantly regretted the harshness.

"I mean, it can't last too long, can it?"

Somebody was walking down the street with a flashlight.

"Who is there?" asked Dog. There was no reply but only hurried footsteps past their trailer.

They slept on the couch, mostly uncomfortable but in each other's arms.

In the morning, Dog woke when Jillian handed him a cup of coffee and she sat down opposite him.

"Are you going to stay and help us?"

"Uh, sure, I suppose," Dog said as if surprised by the question. "Not sure what I can do."

And then he remembered. The big house. The boat. The stocked liquor cabinet.

"Hey, what if we bug out of here and go to a bigger house I know about?"

"Whose house?" she asked. Dog felt suspicion but not because of her question.

"It's a guy I did some work for. He ain't there now, the whole place is empty and we can use it."

"Did he say you could use it?" she plied.

"Kind of, like, well," he paused, "yeah, he won't be around for a while. Snowbird."

"And he said we could use it?"

"Jillian, the dude is gone. He won't be there. He doesn't care. Believe me, he doesn't care if we use the house."

"I can't leave my mom."

"Well, I need to go and check up on it," he said. That liquor cabinet was calling him. "I am going to have a look-see for him and make sure it's all good. Maybe we can go after that."

"Dog, that's fine. But I can't leave Mom."

She was disappointed. *At him*, he thought. *Damn*. He ran his fingers through his greasy hair and rubbed his throbbing head.

"It's okay, Dog, you can go. Can you come back, though?"

"Yeah," he said right away, "I can go and come back."

He began to stand up but she stood faster, pushing him back down.

"After breakfast."

Fifteen minutes and a cigarette later, Dog looked down on a plate of pancakes and a glass of orange drink. He smiled at Jillian as he filled his mouth.

"I could get used to this."

Jillian smiled back and went to the back bedroom to check on her mom.

"She's gone!" He jumped up and instinctively looked for the gun he carried the past few days. It was hidden in the car. He rushed back to the bedroom.

"She's gone!" screamed Jillian. Dog looked down on the bed and squinted in the semi-dark room to see the old lady ashen gray, not moving, her oxygen tubes pushed off the bed and snaking on the floor.

"What the fuck?" Dog started and then Jillian once again screamed something Dog couldn't understand.

Dog walked around the back side of the bed. The oxygen tank was laying on its side, the plastic tubes wrapped up underneath it.

"I think this fell over and pulled her tubes down with it," he said.

Jillian sobbed. Dog stood and walked over to her. He tried to hug her, but she pulled away and once again buried her face in her hands.

What now? Dog wasn't sure. He stood there awkwardly and then thought to check the old lady for any sign of life.

As he felt her wrist, he knew. Cold and already getting stiff. He frowned and tried to feel for a pulse on the side of her neck. Not because he thought there would be a pulse, but because he thought he should do it for Jillian's sake.

He turned to Jillian. She looked at him through the tears.

"Yep," he said with a matter-of-fact tone, "she's gone." Jillian began a new cycle of crying.

Dog sat down on the bed almost touching the dead woman. *Damn. This was all going so well and now she is going to cry all morning.* He sat for a few moments, but his mind kept drifting back to the full liquor cabinet.

"Jill, what do you need me to do here?" He reached out for her again but she pulled away. Yes, the mood had changed. Again.

"Just go," she said. "Just go."

He sighed deeply. If he went, she might be mad. If he stayed, she might keep crying and she seemed mad already. "Damn women," he said to himself.

He stood. "Okay, Jill, I'll be back in a few hours to check up on you."

She said nothing.

21

STAND OFF

Dog opened the front door. Some kids were shooting basketball down the street. Other than that, it looked like a hazy day in Florida.

He opened the door to the Town Car and sat down behind the wheel, leaving one leg on the ground outside the open door. He grabbed the gun from under the carpet. He did not even know what kind it was. He looked at the side of the weapon but lost interest before he read the name. He checked the breach. One bullet in the chamber and one in the magazine. He stuffed it into his waistband and pulled out a cigarette, lit it, and thought about Jillian's mom. He shook his head. *How did that happen?* He thought about how he was a hero last night and today Jillian told him to get out. Damn women. With a clear head but trembling hands, he began to consider his options. Go back to the big house and get some supplies? For sure the old man has jewelry, coins, maybe gold. He must have a couple guns there. There's the booze. That's the short-term plan. What about the long-term? That boat might be the perfect place to weather the next few weeks. A boat like that was designed for living at sea for weeks on end. He could motor out, drop the anchor and not have to worry about anybody else. He'd need some food, booze, and cigarettes first.

Booze. The thought stuck in his head and he pulled up his foot, shut the door, and threw the Lincoln in reverse.

As he backed up and rotated the wheel he took the gun out and laid it on the seat. Bullets. He needed bullets, too. *Damn*, he thought, *where am I going to get all of this stuff?* He cleared the driveway of the trailer court and pulled out onto the main road. There were no cars on the road, but Dog did not notice. He sped up and approached the first stoplight, which was out. He slowed a little, then kept right on going south toward the causeway. Something was across the road ahead and he took his foot off the gas. There was some sort of barricade across the road, and green military vehicles parked to the left and right. A couple uniformed soldiers stood with automatic rifles.

Shit, he thought, *now what?* He slowed to a stop and pulled over. Dog was conditioned to see people in uniforms as hostile. There was no way he would approach them. They would no doubt arrest him for something, what he could not imagine. They'd dream something up. He could not use the gun to force his way through, either. Damn. His mind wandered for a few moments. He slipped the land yacht back into gear and began a slow, looping turn around. As he did, he saw another army vehicle that appeared behind him. It was parked in the middle of the road.

"What the fuck?" he said out loud. He slowed to a stop and squinted at the obstacle, his foot on the brake. There was nothing to do now but continue forward or sit still. He took his foot off the brake and the car slowly began to move forward. As he did, a soldier popped up on top of the Humvee, with an automatic weapon in his hands aimed at Dog. He braked.

Shit. Confused. He sat there. After a minute, he put the car in park. He pulled out a cigarette and fumbled for a lighter. He adjusted his rearview mirror so that he could see the two Humvees behind him. With all three in his sights, he just idled in the air-conditioned vehicle.

After about two minutes that seemed like two hours, the gunner on the Humvee in front of him disappeared. Alarmed, Dog looked up in the mirror. Those soldiers climbed aboard, battening down really fast. They rolled toward him. He pushed himself down in the seat a little, fear taking over. The armored vehicle in front of him whipped a circle. The two behind him passed him, one on each side. All three vehicles headed north and they must have hit 60.

Dog sat still for a few seconds. He noticed that the clock on the dash said 8:45 in crisp green digital numbers. He was not sure what had just happened. *What the hell,* he thought, *time to go.* He jammed back into drive and punched the gas. In a few minutes he was cresting the causeway, the only car on the road. He could not believe his luck. Where had they gone in such a hurry and why? No matter. He came down the causeway and turned south at the first opportunity, cruising into the gate at Ben Thomas's house. The garage door was still up. He pulled in and fumbled for the right button to push on the visor until the door came down. He shut off the car and stepped out.

He stood and stretched. He still had an unlit cigarette hanging from his lips. He went inside and ransacked the kitchen drawers until he found a lighter. He lit up and took a long, steady draw. He exhaled slowly through his nose and took another draw, immediately feeling more relaxed.

First things first. He went to the liquor cabinet and examined the options. He grabbed a bottle of clear whiskey, took the cigarette out of his mouth and gulped down as much as he could.

"Now," he said to nobody, "where is that damn boat?" The *Caruso* rocked gently behind the house, tied fore and aft with large, round buoys protecting her flanks. There was no fence or gate. Dog stepped onto the cement quay and stopped. This was even more than he had imagined. She was perfect. And she was his.

He walked up and looked down in the space between the boat and the cement quay. The buoys rocked gently. He stepped across, raising his leg over the white lifeline and stood on the rough, sandy texture of the top deck. He walked back toward the transom and admired the pilot house. *Damn, can I sail this boat?* He had experience but nothing in this large a vessel. The dinghy that hung on two davits off the stern was the sort of boat he was more confident in.

He walked over to the middle of the cockpit. To the right was the large stainless steel wheel, over two feet in diameter. The control panel mounted above was complicated. Four screens were posted in a semicircle, covered with blue canvas to protect them from the elements. To the left a set of steep steps led up to the flybridge. Dog climbed up part way for a look. Seating, lazarettes, and another, smaller stainless steel wheel. The whole top was encircled with dark blue solar panels.

He retreated and attempted to open the sliding glass door into the recessed saloon. It was locked tight. He did not try to force it. He would get something from the garage to pry open the door. He took a swig, wiped his mouth with the back of his hand and let out a war whoop. *She's a hell of a boat.*

22

COLONEL

"Ma'am, I can't do anything about that now," said the officer.

"These two, sir, put our family in danger," Kate was pointing at the first Humvee that had been on the scene. "They sat there in their little Jeep and did nothing to help us."

"Ma'am, there was a sniper in the area and they were instructed to stay inside the vehicle," the officer said in a monotone.

"Well, they're damn cowards and they threatened to shoot me for helping that wounded soldier."

Dan had walked up and gently placed his hand on her shoulder.

"Kate, we are good, everybody is safe, we should get moving," he said.

"I want to know," demanded Kate, "your name and the names of those two cowards." She was glaring at the officer.

Dan looked at the officer and shrugged his shoulders.

"Ganoe, ma'am, and I am a lieutenant."

"You could help us a little here," Dan suggested. "How about giving us a ride across town?"

"No, I am afraid we can't do that," Ganoe replied. "No civilians in the vehicles. It's a force protection rule and I can't break it."

"Who can?" demanded Kate. Dan smirked and looked admiringly at his wife.

"Ma'am," Ganoe replied, "I am sorry but we are going to have to exfil."

Another Humvee turned onto the 404 and headed their direction. Then another. Then another.

"Aw shit," said Ganoe.

They watched as the small convoy slowed to get a look at the smoke and destruction down the street. They heard the engines rev as the vehicles picked up speed toward them, abruptly stopping in a semi-circle around them. The doors of the first and last vehicle kicked open and soldiers exited both sides, machine guns at the ready. Then the middle vehicle's door opened and a polished boot set down on the pavement.

A tall, lanky man unfolded himself from behind the door and stood. He looked at the squad all around him until he found the highest ranking soldier, who happened to be standing in front of Kate.

"Lieutenant Ganoe, what the hell is going on here?" asked the colonel.

"Sir, we stopped this family, who were armed, and when we did, a sniper shot one of our soldiers," came the crisp reply.

"Bullshit," said Kate. Dan grabbed her arm and she shook him off.

"It's bullshit," she went on. "They stopped us, alright, and left us out in the open. Your soldier got shot and I saved his life. You are very lucky we weren't hurt. You've got some real cowards here."

Dan thought he picked up a faint smirk from the colonel.

"Sir, for all we know, they are coordinating their movements with the sniper," snapped Ganoe.

Dan leaned into Kate, "Cool it," he said under his breath. She glared at him for just a moment and then looked back to the lieutenant. They locked stares.

Ganoe opened his mouth to speak and before he could say anything, the colonel said, "Shut up."

The colonel took a deep breath and frowned. After a few seconds of thought he asked, "Lieutenant, is this family any threat?"

"No sir," he replied slowly. Dipping his head toward Kate he continued, "She rendered medical aid to one of our people and possibly saved his life."

"Then what are we doing here?" asked the colonel.

Ganoe swallowed hard and then said, "Sir, we are going to take these people across town as they have requested, assuming I have your permission, sir."

"You have my permission, let's get moving, I don't like everybody standing out here in the open."

"Yes sir," said Ganoe. He swung around to the original Humvee, "Report to base," he commanded, "and wait for me to return." The big soldier said nothing, no acknowledgment of the command that was made. He turned to get back in the vehicle. The lieutenant's head swung back around toward the colonel and was met with a steely, angry stare.

Shit, the lieutenant thought, shit, shit, shit. Why did his little band of brothers fail to be good soldiers just then?

The colonel shook his head, "I am not impressed."

"Sir, I will handle it, I am sorry sir," he replied.

"Damn right you will handle it," he said as he turned to walk back to his vehicle. He stopped. He turned around in a swift spin.

"Ma'am, thank you for your service to the United States Army. I am sure that soldier will be forever grateful, as will I," he said, looking Kate in the eye.

"It's what I do," she replied, "I am a PA and it's what I do."

"Well, we'll get you where you need to go, but be careful. This mess is only to get worse before it gets better."

"Thank you," she said. "We appreciate your help."

He spun again and disappeared into the vehicle. The convoy spun an arc and left.

"Son of a bitch!" said Ganoe. "Porter!" he called, "You are takin 'em."

The window rolled down, "Yes sir." The window rolled up again.

Kate looked at the lieutenant. "Is that a good idea?" she asked.

He glared and said nothing.

Dan nodded to Kyle and Cooper to pick up the rifles wrapped on the pavement. He walked back toward the vehicle and Ganoe followed his progress with the same iciness he had just given Kate.

"We are taking them with us," said Dan, careful not to give the officer any eye contact.

Dan yanked open the Humvee tailgate. They tossed in their backpacks and placed the rifles on top. Dan picked up Sophie and set her down to one side.

"You sit on this backpack for me, now, okay little girl?" Dan said with a grin. She smiled back and nodded her agreement.

"Cooper, you scramble in back here, too," Dan said.

Kyle, Kate and Dan all got in the back of the armored vehicle. The back seat was shaped in a strange configuration so that the middle seat pushed up, allowing for a gunner to pop the hatch on top and climb into a small tractor-type seat maybe 15 feet above the ground.

The driver punched into gear and they started out.

Porter did not turn around. "I was under orders to stay in the vehicle, ma'am."

Kate said nothing as Dan squeezed her hand. Would she stay quiet?

"I said, I was under orders to stay in the vehicle." Porter's voice was loud and defensive.

The driver said, "Dude, relax."

Porter turned back to look forward. "This is bullshit. We do our jobs and these civvies say we are cowards."

Dan tried to change the subject. "Hey, what's going on in Melbourne?"

Porter stayed silent and the driver asked, "Where are we headed?"

"South through town, along Highway 1, just past Eau Galle about a quarter mile," said Dan.

"We were brought down from Fort Bragg a couple days ago. Our job is to maintain order at night, during the curfew. Perps have made a couple sniper attacks on us. That road you were on has had shooting problems for a couple days. We tracked you in the woods this morning, thinking you might be the threat," the driver said in a mountain twang.

"Tracked us how?" Dan asked.

"Drones, mostly." He held up a tablet computer displaying a moving map. He pointed at the screen and Dan saw Melbourne laid out, with their current location marked in the center, moving like a video game as they drove.

"We picked you up with thermal imaging last night when you walked up to that fence around 4 am."

Dan noted his mistake at the fence. Kate scowled at him, letting go of his hand.

"What's it like in Melbourne right now?" asked Dan again.

"Dangerous. Chaos, really. People should stay inside. Stores are just about empty. No gas. The interstate on the Eastern Seaboard has been shut down for the last couple days. You people are crazy to be out walking around, armed or not," he said.

Finally, Porter spoke. "The Pakistanis set off more nukes. India responded with more of theirs. People are panicking all round the world."

23

RANSACK

Back in the house, Dog made a systematic search. He started in the master bedroom at the back of the first floor. Sliding glass doors overlooking the waterway. You couldn't tell the chaos around coastal Florida outside and what Dog had in mind inside.

He found two tall dressers flanking a smaller one. He started on the left, pulling out each door, moving his hand around the back, sides and bottoms, looking for anything of value. He dumped a few out on the floor but then thought about bringing Jillian here. He didn't want it too messed up. In the first chest of drawers, the woman's, he found nothing of real value. There was a jewelry box, but it contained makeup. There were some photographs and a couple of pieces of jewelry. Dog had no idea if they were worth anything but took whatever might be pawned or bartered.

There was nothing but clothing and some odds and ends in the middle set of drawers. He quickly dispatched these, rifling through them at high speed.

In the final set of drawers he found what he was after. A handgun, with three magazines, all fully loaded. He pulled back the slide. No bullet in the chamber. He racked it once. The weapon surprised him with its silky action. He waved it and took a long look to study its action. "C-Z-something," he said into the empty room, "never heard of it." It was a .40 caliber CZ75 PCR, a quality handgun he had never held before. He stuffed the gun into his waistband and crammed the magazines into his pockets.

In the same drawer he found a few boxes of ammunition, which he set aside reverently on the bed. He sorted through the rest and was about to finish when his hand bumped into something hard. He pulled out a heavy sock, tied in the middle. It clinked when he shook it. He dumped out about twenty gold coins.

"Damn!" he yelled, "now we are talking! Damn African gold!" He piled the coins with the ammunition.

He continued ransacking the ample walk-in closet. The first thing that he saw were the necklaces dangling from a rack on the wall. Most of it was cheap jewelry, but to Dog it was all diamonds and rubies. He found a canvas tote filled with more totes. He dumped them out and poured in ten pounds of jewelry. He scraped some rings out of a ring box and threaded them onto a single necklace. He pushed back the clothes that were hanging into the back of the closet. Nothing.

Above his head were boxes. He reached up and took one down. Opening it, he found clothes. It looked like a wedding dress to him, all folded neatly in a plastic bag. He dropped that box and took another, only to find it filled with photos. After a few more boxes, he gave up on the closet.

He dumped the ammunition and gold into the tote and turned around for a final look. His eyes caught something behind the curtain leaned up against the wall. Something long and black. He pulled back the curtain: a Remington 870 shotgun. It was the tactical version with a short barrel mostly used for home defense.

"Double damn!" he shouted. Picking up the shotgun he racked it once. A shell ejected and flew across the room. He could not find the shell. He carefully opened the chamber and saw that a new shell had taken its place. He slid the chamber shut and grabbed his loot, scrambling down the hall.

The doorbell rang.

Dog stopped dead still. The doorbell rang again.

The front door was some 40 feet away. Down the hallway and to the left. Dog listened for a clue. His sweat turned icy.

The bell rang twice. It was the sound of impatience.

Dog tried to remember how he had entered the house. Through the front door? No - the garage. But he hadn't locked the front door, either. For all he knew, it had been unlocked since his first visit.

The door handle clicked. Dog heard the familiar sucking sound of the seal as the door slowly opened and was pushed in.

Dog shuffled quietly a few feet forward. Ahead of him, but in sight of the entryway, was a window. He wanted to look out and see what kind of vehicle had arrived.

"Ben?" came the squeaky voice of an elderly woman, "are you here? It's just me."

Dog slowly lowered the tote bag onto the floor. He gripped the shotgun with two hands. He froze, thinking better of taking the offensive. He picked up the tote again and slowly retreated back toward the bedroom with the shotgun pointed down the hallway.

"Ben, I am a little scared," he heard the voice call out. "Where are you?"

Somebody walking toward the kitchen. He advanced down the hallway once again leaving the bag behind. The door was wide open.

"Ben, are you in the back?"

The woman turned the small lever that locked the sliding glass door. He moved toward the window in the hallway as the door slid slowly on its racers.

A yellowing fiberglass golf cart stood in the middle of the driveway loop. Most every old person in Florida had one or knew someone who did.

He inhaled for the first time in what seemed like a long minute and walked backwards slowly toward the bedroom.

The glass door shut with a metallic click. Small feet slid across tile and stopped, just in front of the living room entrance. Dog held his breath.

He wondered why he was hiding. He had the gun. It was just an old woman. Was it because he was stealing? He wasn't sure. He waited for another few seconds and was just settling on a course of action. He heard movement again.

She clomped toward the front door. She paused for a moment and then he heard it shut. He strained his ears and heard the almost silent golf cart start up and move out.

Dog started breathing again, picked up the treasure tote and walked back toward the liquor cabinet. He stopped in front of the kitchen counter and noticed, for the first time, a red line of blood moving from the living room to the back door and out the house.

"Damn."

24

REPORT

Clara Morgan shook like a palm tree in a Florida hurricane. Her hand trembled so hard she could barely steer the golf cart. She was not a forensics expert but it did not take much expertise to figure out what had happened at the Thomas place. She had forced herself to follow the trail of blood in case Ben or Claire were hurt and needed help. That blood trail went all the way to the waterfront.

Claire and Clara. They had been a pair for so many years. They saw themselves as the geriatric version of Thelma and Louise. So many nights playing cards with the Thomases over the years. They had cruised together, driven to Branson for the shows and watched each other's little dogs. When Clara's husband developed cancer, it was Claire who was there for her, day and night until he passed. Then, as Claire began to fall victim to Alzheimer's, it was Clara's turn to be her light. Ben was a good man but it was too much for anybody to handle alone.

Clara aimed her electric vehicle down the center of Riverside Drive. Not a car in sight. She had not ventured out for a few days but had grown concerned when her calls to Ben went unanswered. Then, when the phone went out, she made the short drive. They had been neighbors but soon after her husband grew sick they had downsized into a waterfront condo. It was lovely but for the rowdy bar down the beach that played music until late. But that was a small price to pay to be close to friends. She was not heading home now, though. Her condo passed on the right. She was heading to the Indianatlantic Town Police Station on 5th Street.

As her bony fingers tightened on the plastic steering wheel, she thought about what she had seen. Somebody had been hurt. Maybe worse. As soon as she had pushed open the door she knew something was wrong. Ben would not leave the door unlocked. When she saw the blood, she knew there was no choice. She had to check out back for Ben and Claire. It had taken everything in her to go out the sliding glass door. She stopped and turned around when the blood led down to the canal. The boat swayed gently tied up to the pier and nobody was in sight. She walked gingerly through this loving house that now seemed to be a crime scene.

Now she was so afraid she could barely grip the steering wheel.

How far was it? She had been there so many times but now she was having trouble navigating. She focused on driving. Still no cars on the road, no people whatsoever. She slowed down slightly and looked over at the houses on the right. In the first one a man stood behind a glass door looking out with something long in his hand. A rifle? She pressed back down on the accelerator. People were sheltering at home but they were not outside.

She rehearsed what she would say to the police. What could she tell them that would get them to respond? She settled on the straight up facts. "If something had happened, they would have let me know." She thought about the options. Maybe they traveled to see their son and an animal had gotten into the house. That was a little far-fetched and she knew it. Where else could they have gone? Violence took them. She had no other answer.

Just ahead was 5th Street. A half-dozen olive drab and tan military vehicles parked on the road to the right, evidently guarding the bridge. She slowed down and wondered if she should just talk with them. Then she gunned the engine.

She turned onto 5th Street, almost tipping the golf cart as she clipped the curb to get up on the sidewalk. Her nerves began to settle. Two and a half blocks to the police station. Suddenly, there were more military vehicles blocking the road. Silhouettes of a couple armed men stood on alert dressed in military fatigues. Now she was very confused.

She slowed at the roadblock. An MP stepped forward and held up his gloved hand.

"Stop!" he yelled, "Do not approach!"

Claire stopped. She sat in the golf cart, both hands on the wheel with an indignant and angry look.

The MP had an M16 slung over his shoulder with the barrel pointing down toward the ground but ready to swing into action.

As he got close she noticed for the first time that the vehicles behind him had armed men on top with large swiveling guns aimed at her.

"I am going to the police station," she said. He was just a few feet away. He tilted his weapon slightly.

"Ma'am, exit the vehicle," he ordered in a Georgia accent.

"I will not!" she exclaimed, "I am here to report a murder."

"Ma'am, I am sorry, but normal local police operations are currently suspended. We do not have the capacity to handle civilian police duties. Do you have identification?"

"No, I don't have identification! I am here to report a murder, young man." she said glaring at him, "Are you going to do something about it?" She pointed her bony index finger at his face.

"Ma'am, please exit the vehicle and I will see what we can do here."

Claire reached down to shift the transmission from forward to reverse.

"Ma'am!" shouted the soldier, "Show me your hands!" He stepped back and brought his weapon up to sit squarely inches from her face.

Claire threw her hands up in the air and began to shake uncontrollably. She shrieked, her hands nervously twitching in the air.

The soldier grabbed her thin, frail arm. He tugged it and with one motion swung the 104-pound woman out of the golf cart. She could not get her feet under her as the motion stopped and she fell to her knees, her arm snapping in the grip of the soldier. She screamed in pain as another soldier yelled, "Clear!" from the far side of the golf cart as he aimed his weapon at Claire's body.

She passed out from the pain in the oil-stained parking lot.

25

WAREHOUSE

D an looked at his wife as she stared outside the front window of the Humvee. He had seen this side of her before but never quite to this level. He wondered what would have been had she not taken the initiative. She had kept her grief bottled up and then it blew. He looked forward as they approached a checkpoint and the vehicle slowed.

Two soldiers approached the vehicle while Porter rolled down his window. It only went down about two inches.

"Colonel's orders," yelled Porter.

"Yeah, we know," said one of the soldiers standing up tall to look into the backseat. "We just wanted to see the woman who kicked your ass." They laughed as Porter rolled his window back up and they moved forward.

Dan smiled inwardly and then offered, "News travels fast here."

"Yeah, lots of radio chatter, I am sure," said the driver.

The vehicle skidded to a stop.

"Looters," said the driver. They all strained to look forward. A gang of a half-dozen thuggish looking young people ran across the road, overloaded with merchandise and food and liquor, disappearing between buildings up ahead.

"They scattered when they saw us coming," said Porter. "I hope you have a good place to hunker down."

The armored attack vehicle took off again.

"We do," said Dan, "but we have one stop to make before we get there, and we will be safe until then."

Kate looked at Dan and asked, "Do you really think it is safe?"

"Yes, we should be good. I have a couple backup plans until we get on the boat."

"The boat?" asked Porter. "You are going on a boat?"

Dan realized his mistake and said nothing. It was quiet for a few moments.

"Hey, we can get out of here," said Dan.

"Here?" asked the driver, looking at an industrial strip.

"Yep, we rent two of these units right here," replied Dan.

They rolled to a stop.

Dan stepped down as Kate got out on the other side and they helped the two smallest kids down. Kyle was handing backpacks and wrapped weapons down to Dan and Kate. Porter popped open his door but stayed seated.

"Let's make sure we don't see you again," said Porter, "You really shouldn't be keeping those rifles."

"We'll stay out of sight," said Dan, who had dropped to one knee and was pulling a remote control from his backpack.

"That's not going to work," said Porter, "no electricity."

"Yeah," replied Dan not looking up, "it's for the generator." He pressed it and an unseen engine cranked up.

Porter looked at Dan with a quizzical face. "A generator inside? That sounds like a winner. Y'all be dead shortly."

"Don't worry," said Dan, "it's on the roof. It's just to get the battery system charged up and when it is running," he said standing up and clicking the remote again, "I can open the door."

Dan turned to Porter, "Thanks for the lift and I hope your boy makes it without any serious complications."

Porter nodded, slammed his door and they sped off as the family entered the warehouse.

Dan surveyed the mostly empty room. "Looks like nobody got here first, so that's good news." As soon as they were all in, he lowered the door. The roof of the bays had white plastic skylights. There was a gray Zodiac inflatable boat with a rigid wooden deck on an aluminum trailer. A two-person camo-color ATV was behind the boat with a tarp thrown over it. Two shipping containers were pushed up against each of the walls. The unit was equipped with power tools and emergency equipment. A couple large rolling tool sets were pushed against the walls alongside a drill press, a band saw and other power tools. An office with a full bathroom had been built to one side. A large glass window overlooked the warehouse from the office as if made for a boss to sit inside and watch the employees work. The office had a railing encircling its top with a simple kitchenette, furniture and a TV covered by a large tarp. Rough stairs provided access. The middle of the expansive room was mostly empty. Dan had planned their survival staging area well.

"Home for a few days," said Dan as the door banged shut.

He looked at Kate. She grinned and said, "First shower."

Dan smiled back. "That's great, you go. I'll turn on the water and make sure nobody has been in here. Kyle, please collect and empty the rifles. Stack them on the table in a safe manner. You know how to do that."

Kyle glanced at Cooper and then back at his dad with an imploring look.

"Don't worry about Cooper, just do it," said Dan.

"Cooper," said Dan while handing him a set of keys, "unlock the containers and get the gun cleaning equipment out. The three of us will clean and prep all the weapons. As soon as your mom and Sophie are done showering, we will each take a turn getting the stink off of us."

Cooper took the keys and marched off.

Dan checked the rear corner of the bay. There was a wellhead sitting on top of a barrel. A hole in the cement allowed a pipe for well water. Next to the barrel was a workbench covered in 12 volt batteries. Dan unplugged a lead to the roof and connected it to a solar cell. He then pushed a test button and a voltmeter gave him the system power level. Full power. So far so good. He plugged another lead in, powering the whole system inside the warehouse. The water pump took off immediately and began pushing water up onto a black barrel that stood on the rooftop. Everybody would have water for a shower but the last couple might get cold water.

Kyle was stripping off his boots. Cooper did likewise and the three of them were soon sitting at the picnic table, cleaning weapons.

"Dad," Cooper asked, "how long is it going to be like this?"

"I don't know, Coop. Some people say that when something bad happens like we are experiencing, there will be a short time of adjustment, maybe a few weeks or months, before the government is in control again." "But Dad," said Kyle, "they are talking about nuclear winter. That could last for years."

"That could be true," said Dan, "It looks like they are moving pretty fast, so maybe it will be shorter. Pass that gun oil, please." He squirted some onto a rag. "This is uncharted territory for the whole world. Most of what we have seen here in the US is the result of people acting out of fear. I am sure that some of the best scientific minds are thinking through what this all means. We need to focus on being smart and as self sufficient as possible."

"Dad," asked Cooper, "what if our boat is gone when we show up tomorrow?"

"We're not going to worry about things we can't control, Coop. But not many people can handle a big cat like ours."

Deep inside Dan shared the same fear. What if the boat was gone? He'd take a look for himself.

26

RECONNAISSANCE

S oon, they had the guns stored, everybody had showered, and Kate and Cooper were cooking. They were all wearing light clothing, better suited to the heat. Fortunately, it was still a mild Florida spring, early in the year, and comfortable.

Dan was straining to hear any practical news he could find on the shortwave receiver. The same emergency broadcast notice replayed in an endless loop. A few ham radio operators, part of the emergency relay network, tried to make connections around the globe. A few other stations were broadcasting because he could faintly make them out. Somebody in the military, however, had decided to jam the airwaves to control what news could get through.

He thought about the next phase of his plan. He needed to make sure the boat was there and then figure out how to ferry supplies. A few boatloads would finish stocking the vessel for the trip. He had the Zodiac for that and the ATV to pull it down the street to the landing. Could he do that? Would he be allowed to do so? It was time to venture out.

He grabbed his go bag, packed night-vision goggles, a couple cartons of cigarettes and a box of ammunition. He found a pair of high-powered binoculars, purchased on an auction site. He wondered if that site was still in business. Then he thought about the internet itself and wondered how it was functioning. Probably, he mused, because it entertained people, helped them to relax and kept them communicating. Even if it was laced with propaganda.

He went to the gun safe and took out a 9 mm Glock. He had shot it thousands of times but now it felt different in his hand. It was a deadly weapon, not meant for practice anymore.

Kate was standing with her hands on her hips, staring at him.

"You aren't going out there," she said flatly.

"I have to," he said. "We need to know how to get supplies to the boat."

"Can we have one night here, just us, with no guns and running around?"

He stalled, inhaled and gathered his thoughts.

"Each day we stay ashore we are in more danger. It's going to be safer out on the water," he said, enveloping her in his arms. "I need to make sure the boat is intact, that we can get more supplies over to it, and that it's safe to take our kids."

She looked at him, expressionless. She was weighing his response but also preparing her protest. She looked away, tears brimming on her eyes and he hugged her harder.

"Stop it," she said, pushing him away. "You are so black and white. All of this has happened and you just go on like everything is fine."

He backed off a step. It was true and false. It was true that he was black and white. For Dan, life was filled with certainty, cause, effect and consequence. It was his strength and it was a weakness. But it was not true that he was acting as if everything was fine. Quite the opposite.

"Okay," he said, "let's have dinner as a family. I'll head out later. I need to go."

She did not reply, but had already turned to go upstairs toward the small kitchenette. Dan retreated to the office and sat down at the metal desk. He unlocked the file cabinet and took out a set of provisioning lists that he had drawn up some months before. He started a new list now, highlighting what was on the boat already, what they had here in the containers and what they were going to have to do without. He listed chores for the boys.

Dan prepped for his reconnaissance mission. He was dressed in jeans, a loose t-shirt and had a small black backpack slung over his shoulder. He wore a baseball cap, hiking sandals and looked a lot like another Florida tourist, ready for a day of walking through Melbourne. He hid a handgun holstered on his right hip, covered by the loose shirt, a hunting knife on his left side. "Back in a few hours," he told Kate as he kissed her. She did not return his affection.

"Just be safe." Sophie clung to his leg as he reminded the boys that they were to work off the list before bed.

"Nobody comes in, Kate," he reminded her.

Stepping out into the late afternoon sun, Dan put on his sunglasses and walked down the sidewalk. His goal was to be nobody special, blend in and to simply go about his business. He needed information and that meant contact with people. That was the most dangerous part of his mission. First, though, he was going to look across the Indian River and see if their floating home was okay.

It was another hazy day. A slight salty breeze wafted in from the Atlantic, accented by musky mangroves. He headed north on Highway 1 towards 192, with a plan to cut east toward the waterfront. He saw pedestrians ahead, most with the heads down and moving with purpose as if on errands. No cars. Ahead, across the street and to the right, was The Last Chance bar and grill. He could get an update about the current conditions and barroom rumors. Plenty of daylight left and he could look for the boat later.

A couple of cars in the parking lot signaled this business was open. A hand painted sign hung on the door with the words "WE SHOOT LOOTERS" in white letters on a black background. The door jangled with a bell, announcing his presence. A wall of cold air hit him. There must be a generator around, he thought, but in reality, the power was still on in this neighborhood.

Two older men sat like clay fixtures on high barstools. Behind the bar, a tattooed, smoking bartender leaned against the cash register. A shotgun stood on its butt, leaning behind him. All six eyes focused on

Dan, narrowing because of the light streaming in behind. Dan removed his sunglasses, flashed a cautious smile, strode up the bar and sat down, dropping his backpack onto his lap. A large TV showed a news station but the volume was off.

The bartender said nothing, and looked at Dan waiting for him to place an order.

"Miller, please," said Dan.

"All we got is cans. Ten bucks." The bartender didn't move.

He reached in his backpack and, keeping the wad of money inside, peeled off a ten-dollar bill. He dropped it on the bar.

The bartender reached into a chest refrigerator, grabbed a glass and a can and set them down in front of Dan. He picked up the bill. The whole time he kept his eyes on Dan.

Down the bar, Dan heard somebody say something under his breath. The only word he could make out was "asshole."

27

INTELLIGENCE

Dan sipped his beer. Then he decided on the direct approach. He looked up at the bartender, then down the bar.

"I just walked up from Vero. Is there any news that I should be aware of?"

Nobody said a word. A long uncomfortable pause. Dan looked at the flat screen. As if reading his mind, the bartender said, "We're sick of the same damn news."

The man in the Raiders t-shirt and black knee socks sitting closest to him cleared his throat. Without looking down at Dan, he said, "Yeah, the damn world's falling apart."

Dan nodded in agreement. Silence in the bar. The bartender began washing some glasses. It appeared he was washing glasses that were already clean.

"Who's in charge here? The cops or the military?" Dan ventured.

The same man who had spoken before said, "The military. There is a curfew on, and they enforce it. Since we are so close to the air force base here, they have plenty of people. With guns." The other man finally spoke up. "How did you get here from Vero without knowing that?"

Dan looked down the bar at him and he stared back, challenging Dan to answer. For the first time, Dan noticed that he was younger, more fit, and was sporting a Gold's Gym t-shirt. If there was trouble, and there might be, this was the guy to watch out for.

"Things are different in different places," Dan said, "last night I saw a lot of Air Force and Army guys on the highway. Didn't know if they were leaving or just passing through."

"There is curfew on," said Gold's Gym, "What are you doing out at night?"

"I got stuck between towns and had to sleep out under the stars," said Dan. The room fell silent again.

Just as Dan was about to down his beer and leave, the door jangled opened. A tanned, bearded man dressed in biker's black and leather, strode in. He smiled and stopped after making a step or two inside.

"Hey!" he said loudly, "where's the Norm?" he asked. He held his arms open with a questioning face. Nobody said anything.

"Well, damn," he said, pausing for effect and the man yelled out, "Norm!" Dan knew he was referring to a 1980s sitcom in which everybody at the bar would yell "Norm" when a particular patron walked in.

"Hey Art," said Norm as he took a seat alongside the two, closest to Dan. The bartender said, "Hey Norm."

Norm thumped the bar and asked, "What are you charging today?"

The bartender responded, "10 bucks for a beer, 20 for a shot. No food and no credit. No shit."

"Shit! That's robbery," said Norm, "gimme a beer." He walked over to Gold's Gym and slapped him on the back. "Speaking of shit, Mac, you look like it." Norm laughed and Mac nodded his head and mouthed, "very funny."

Norm feigned tipping his hat toward Dan. Dan nodded in return and flashed him a muted smile. The bartender set a beer down on the bar and waited for Norm to pay up.

"Any cigarettes to be had?" asked Norm.

The bartender shook his head.

"Well," said Norm, "what's happening around here?"

The bartender shrugged and still did not speak. Finally, Gold's Gym said, "It's bad, Norm, but you should be telling us what's happening."

As if waiting for the opportunity, Norm's bass voice filled the room.

"I did a run up to Jacksonville last night," he replied. "Hundreds of trucks, all escorted by the National Guard. Their plan is to keep the big box stores stocked and federalized. They federalized the fuel system, so all gas stations that have fuel have to work with us truckers."

"Federalized?" Gold's Gym interrupted.

"Uncle Sam takes over. Government is in charge. Stores will be operating 24/7 until the bureaucrats give 'em a break. Truckers like me are driving on a credit system. If we drive, we get paid but not until the feds are ready to release the cash to us. A couple of guys said no and had their rigs taken."

"How the fuck?" the bartender interrupted.

"You going to say 'no' to the US Army? They got the distribution centers, too. That's where I started from last night and that's where I will be tonight." He swigged beer.

Dan was listening intently. It made sense. Hungry people will panic without food. And fuel. The government had to repair the supply chains across the country before more chaos turned into riots, looting and bloodshed. They had just a few days before chaos ensued.

"So how are you getting gas?" asked Raiders Man.

"Like I said, some gas stations are federalized. MPs check everybody's papers when they pull off the exits. I saw a guy get taken down last night. He walked into the station with a gas can and started arguing. They put him down on the ground and cuffed him. While I was fueling up, a truck pulled up with about a dozen people in the back, all tied up, all angry lookin'."

Norm shook his head.

"I gassed up this morning down at Patrick. It's really crazy down there." He took a swig of his beer and looked at Dan.

"You live here?"

"Nope," replied Dan as casually as he could, "Just passing through."

"Says he came in from Vero last night," said Gold's Gym.

"Not likely," said Norm staring at Dan, "that route is locked down at night."

Dan, immediately on the defensive, felt it best to tell some of the truth. "The military brought us in."

Norm set his beer down on the bar and turned to Dan.

"What do you mean, by *brought us in*?"

"My wife is a doctor of sorts and she helped them, so they helped us," Dan replied.

Norm took another swig, "I suppose that's possible. Lots of accidents, shootings, lootings. A doctor would be a big help."

Dan opened up his backpack on the bar to avoid arousing suspicion. He withdrew a pack of cigarettes. He slid them down the bar. Norm stopped the sliding pack of cigarettes with his right hand.

"I don't want any trouble," said Dan "but I am interested in what's happening. I am trying to get my family across the causeway bridge. We haven't heard any real news for about three days."

Norm began opening up the cigarettes. "It's pretty simple. Four days ago the banks were frozen. Three days ago they slapped a curfew into place. Two days ago they lost control of a bunch of major cities."

"Whereabouts?" asked Dan.

"They decided to drop the military on people in hardcore fashion. Here in Florida, Miami, Tampa and Tallahassee are under shoot-to-kill orders. Orlando has not been as bad, but just about any major city is almost a war zone."

"Wow," said Dan.

"For some reason, Jacksonville is the worst. Nobody can get in or out. They're stockpiling stuff just south of town until things settle down. Yesterday they started moving goods using the Air Force and National Guard and civilian truck drivers like me. Here in Brevard

County you had better be careful if you plan on walking around at night."

"Is it okay to be out during the day?"

"The authorities will mostly leave you alone but good people have become desperate. There is talk of a militia that is trying to fight the government. Rebels. Outlaws. Just west of here, before you get to Orlando, some group has organized and they shut down 192, 520 and 50."

Dan felt the hair on his neck rise.

"Rumor is that we might see quite a bit of action in the skies over there tonight."

Norm took a sip. He looked at Dan and said gravely, "Some people will kill you for your pack of smokes."

Dan stood and took out another pack of cigarettes, tossing them to Norm.

"Thanks, brother, I appreciate it," he said, and walked out into the heat of a day slowly losing its grip, giving way to a sky turning a deep gold.

He was spooked.

28

OFFICER

Officer Phillip Nolan sat back in his office chair in a sour mood. He had been cooped up now for almost thirty-six hours by the military and he was getting peeved. The chief had not come in since last week and Nolan, though way down the seniority list, was the acting commander. It was only because he had been on duty when the Army rolled in and took over his town.

After a day of doing nothing but handing over keys and showing them how to use the radios and other gear, he sent the staff home. He could get them back if needed, but for now, there was nothing to do except wait.

He stood and rolled his head, popping his neck. He split the window blind slats to look out at the checkpoint in front of the station. It was the same setup today, just a different set of eighteen-year-olds. To the west the heat steamed from the pavement. He squinted at a yellowed golf cart coming down the road. He let go of the slats and searched for his binoculars. "Well, what do you know?" he said under his breath. It was Clara Morgan. He laughed out loud. *Those army boys are in trouble now*, he thought. She rolled down the road, at full tilt for a golf cart, and saw a soldier with an M16 machine gun in front of her. His anger grew as he saw the big weapons mounted on top of the vehicles swivel over toward her.

"Morons," he said into the empty room.

Clara was in all her busybody glory as he had seen her many times before. She had called the station for noisy neighbors, noisy cats, noisy cars and noisy beach parties. The Noise Queen. She had called when her neighbor had parked a few inches on her grass and then again when he had not been home for a few days (he had gone on a trip up north). She had called and called for just about any reason. Nolan and his officers knew her well.

He laughed again when her bony hand came up and pointed at the young sentry's face. He had been pointed at himself too many times to count.

He stopped laughing, though, when the young man reached over and yanked her from the cart. She flipped out of the cart like a rag doll and flopped on the pavement. It happened so fast that Nolan did not react until it was over.

He rushed out past the front desk and out onto the sidewalk. He strode forward to the rear of the checkpoint where a soldier stood craning his neck to see the action on the sidewalk about fifty feet away.

"I am going over there. I know that lady," said Nolan.

"Sir, you can't do that, I am sorry. But let me check with the sergeant," he replied.

He spoke into a microphone clipped to his shirt, "Sarge, we have a situation here and the policeman knows that subject on the ground." There was a moment of silence as the soldier listened via his earpiece. "Go for it, man, no problem."

Nolan walked up to Clara and two soldiers stooped down. They were trying to determine what was wrong. Nolan could see that her arm was bent in a strange way.

"Get back, you idiots," he said, his anger bubbling over. They complied immediately.

She was breathing but he instinctively looked for a pulse.

"There is a first aid kit behind the reception desk in the station.

Go get it. And there is a refrigerator with ice packs in the break room. Get those," he ordered the closest soldier.

"You go get the board for carrying people," he commanded. "It is hanging on the wall down the main hallway."

Neither soldier moved.

"We can't leave this post, sir. But let me radio for some help," he said.

"Fine," Nolan responded, "get a damn ambulance on the way, too."

Ten minutes later they were carrying Clara into the air-conditioned police station. Her arm was wrapped in ice and an ambulance was on the way. They set her down gently on the floor of the reception area.

Nolan sat next to her and waited. Her breathing was regular but shallow. He felt her forehead and all seemed well.

After about five minutes, her eyes fluttered open and she looked at Nolan.

"Officer Nolan," she stammered, pausing to breathe deeply. "Praise God, it's Officer Nolan."

"Hey Mrs. Morgan, just sit still, we are going to get you to the hospital."

"Officer Nolan, Ben and Claire Thomas. You have to go check on them. They were murdered," she whispered in a song-song voice.

"Why do you think that? Did you see it happen?"

"No, but I know they were killed. There was blood. A trail to the water. Ben would not leave her side. Something is terribly wrong. Please go."

"Okay, Mrs. Morgan. Let's make a deal. You relax, just relax until the ambulance gets here. If you do, I'll go check on the Thomas house as soon as I can," he said in a sincere voice.

"Oh, thank you, Officer Nolan, thank you," she looked straight up at the ceiling and was quiet for a moment. Then she turned back to Nolan and said, "Check the backyard. There is something in the backyard."

"Okay, Mrs. Morgan, now just relax." Nolan searched for a topic of discussion other than the Thomas house and murders.

"Mrs. Morgan, I am going to take your golf cart back to your house."

"Thank you," she said breathlessly. "Thank you. But check on the Thomases first, okay?"

"Okay," he replied with a little chuckle, "I'll do that first."

The ambulance arrived and they loaded Clara. As Nolan looked in through the back doors, she struggled to sit up.

"You said you would go," she said in her feeble voice.

"Yes, ma'am, I did and I will do my best to check on the Thomas house, just like you asked."

"There is blood in the living room, too!" she said, again in a muted shout.

"Okay, Mrs. Morgan, I will look into it," said Nolan, "now you focus on getting better and I will see you when things settle down around here."

He stepped back and the doors of the ambulance swung shut. Nolan spun around and asked the nearest sentry. "Who is the commanding officer here?"

"That would be Sergeant Monroe, sir."

"Where is he?" asked Nolan, "I want to ask him how many more old ladies we are going to be going to war with today."

The soldier pointed toward an older NCO standing back by a set of loudly humming generators. Nolan stomped off toward him, intent on telling the US Army why there was a police force. When he got to the guardhouse, he was denied entry and told to stand down.

29

PREPARATIONS

Dog knew that before he could bring Jillian back here he would have to clean up the place. Otherwise, she would get suspicious. He did not want her asking questions that would make him feel guilty. He knew she would.

He finally found a bucket and mop in the laundry room. He began in the living room where he had killed Ben Thomas. The blood had dried and the stain was stubborn. As he scrubbed, he spread the area larger, got more water, used more towels and soon had a pile of dirty laundry. He moved from the living room into the kitchen and to the sliding glass doors. When he finished indoors, he put the laundry in the garbage can, then washed away most of the blood on the porch and sidewalk.

Satisfied that he had cleaned things up enough, he checked other parts of the house. Not until he was completely done did he take out another bottle of alcohol. He poured himself a glass of vodka and realized he was hungry. There was not much in the refrigerator. He found some pastrami and ate it straight out of the plastic container. There were eggs but Dog was not into cooking. Making sandwiches, he began to think about the situation. The snoopy old lady was probably going to find the cops and they would investigate sooner or later.

The best thing he could do was to leave for a while and then come back. He had to find Jillian anyway. He thought about the car, the road and the checkpoints. He couldn't cross the bridge again.

What about the boat out back? Could he cross over in the boat? It was a big boat and it was probably pretty complicated. The Indian River was shallow. Rocks, shoals, oyster bars. It would be hard enough to learn how to sail an unknown boat without that complication. He did not need a boat that big. Then it dawned on him that a dinghy was tied up, hanging on davits. It was the ship's tender.

The tender was small but big enough for a couple of people. It had a sturdy 40-horse outboard motor, the type that Dog had plenty of experience using. All he had to do was lower it in the water and off he'd go. It was late afternoon already. In another few hours, it would be dark and he could cut straight across the water to Riverview Park. He could walk a mile or two to Jillian's house from there. He missed her warmth.

Could he afford to wait an hour or two? Risky. It had already been a while since the old lady had left. How long until somebody showed up? All of a sudden, an icy feeling of fear crept over Dog. While he had been going about this business, time worked against him. It always did. There could be a dozen cops outside the front door right now. What the hell was he doing?

He stood and stole across the kitchen, staying out of the line of sight from the front windows. He shuffled into the hallway between the living room and kitchen, near the front door. He stole a glance. Nobody. He relaxed some, and then took a good long look. Nobody was out front. He was brave enough to slip into the garage and put down the garage door. He walked out front. The gate was wide open.

He shut the gate and locked the front door.

Back in the kitchen he sorted his emergency supplies on the table. The unfinished bottle of vodka, the two handguns, the shotgun and the tote with the ammunition and gold jewelry from the bedroom. The shotgun? He thought better about bringing it. He could not walk around Melbourne with a shotgun. He leaned the gun up against the wall, just around the corner. Back to the kitchen and the pile. No way he could take it all. He pulled out the first handgun and checked it. Two bullets. He chambered one and made sure it was ready to fire. He looked around the kitchen and with a shrug, opened the refrigerator. He placed the weapon on the top shelf next to a carton of skim milk. He unloaded some of the ammunition, setting the boxes on the table.

What about taking a shower? His arm pulsed down over his elbow. He picked at the bandage and wanted to remove it and then clean it. The sun had sunk on the horizon. This added to his sense of urgency. Skip the shower.

He stuck Ben's handgun into this beltline and pulled his shirt down. He noticed the blood splatter on his shirt. So would everyone else. He stashed the vodka into the bag, gulped the glass and felt the warm flush of another sundown, and exited the back of the house. He pulled the sliding glass door shut and stepped toward the sailboat with the canvas tote in his left hand.

The slightest breeze wafting in from the Atlantic created a slight chop. The sky was golden and Dog relished the spectacular Florida sunset, maybe a half-hour of daylight. Maybe it would be a good day after all. As he neared the sailboat, he stopped to look down at the space between the cement quay and the boat.

Ben Thomas was there.

His body was floating up by the surface, small catfish nibbling at the body.

It did not make sense. There was a tidal flow in the Indian River. He had grown up here, watching the water rush back and forth. Somehow, this little protected spot had created an eddy that had trapped the body here. Nothing he could do about it, though, so he stepped onto the boat and walked aft.

Two stainless steel arms extended off the stern. Angled upward, two nylon ropes were tied fore and aft holding the dinghy aloft. The dinghy was a 12-foot semi-rigid boat with a 40-horsepower outboard.

There was a rope brake on the right steel arm and Dog could see that this was where the rope must be set free to lower the dinghy. He tossed the treasure tote into the small boat. He'd figure it out. How hard could this be?

Without securing the rope to the winch, Dog flipped the lever on the rope brake straight up. The arms slammed down and the dinghy hit the water at an odd angle, falling about eight feet with a splash. The heavier stern end was in the water and the lighter bow stuck up a few feet above the water. The engine was dangerously low in the water.

"Damn," said Dog. He scrambled for the rope. A turn in the rope had stopped the arms from falling their entire distance and now was wedged up against the brake.

He grasped the loose end in two hands and pulled as hard as he could, unable to budge it. He could see the danger at hand. If the water got any higher on the motor he would be going nowhere. He scrambled up to the house and sprinted back with a large kitchen knife.

He slashed the rope and the boat settled flat on the surface. Dog jumped in and loosened the ropes holding the dinghy to the catamaran. He flipped on the safety switch, primed the gas by pumping a black bulb and pulled on the starter cord. The little motor sprang to life on the first pull. Dog pushed away and aimed due west toward the mainland. He wanted to hold Jillian again.

30

NOBODY HOME

N olan sat down at his desk and considered his options. He wrote down all the names he could remember of the military personnel who had so obscenely hurt the old lady. He knew details would grow sketchy so he added the date and time. He jotted a few more things to jog his memory and picked up his phone to see if it was working. It was not. The military had redirected all incoming calls to their own switchboard and in the process knocked the station's phone offline. He slammed the phone down and stood.

It was bad police work to go back to the Thomas house alone. He needed backup. He did not believe the old lady but he had made a promise and he was going to keep it. He did not interview her properly. She had made no formal missing persons report. He had no photo, no discovery document, no partner, and no orders. What if he found bodies after all this? If she was right, precious minutes were mounting, making any forensic work more difficult. He could not sit around any more.

In the rear of the station were old radios for events, crowd management and a few other odd responsibilities. He grabbed two. Exiting the police station, he looked at the row of parked police cars. They were off-limits due to the police stand-down ordered by the military. His anger boiled up just like his blood pressure. Did these idiots not understand the difference between an army, whose job was to take and occupy enemy territory, and a town police force? He was disgusted beyond words.

Clara's white golf cart sat out front. He climbed aboard and reached down to put it into reverse and it beeped. He did not ask permission and nobody was going to bother with him. He spun in an arc, then switched to forward and bucked off the sidewalk back onto the road. His first stop would be an apartment a few blocks north near the Thomas house.

He hoped nobody was watching as he sped off, but it was a golf cart and not a squad car. He rolled north on Riverside and then hung a right and pulled into a set of low, single story condos. He went up to the second in the row of houses and knocked.

Stacie Raisch opened the door. She was twenty-eight years old, a single mom, and the newest member of the force hired two years prior. At the time, Nolan had felt that if they were doing the affirmative action thing, it should have been a Hispanic hire. Instead, they had opted for a divorced woman who spoke some Spanish. Then he was partnered with her. At the time it felt like a punishment. Now, he looked forward to any excuse to patrol with her.

At first she didn't reciprocate any interest in Nolan, afraid that it could jeopardize her job. Now, after two years of working together, they had grown used to each other and shared respect. He had come to see her as the most thorough and conscientious officer on the small force. He had watched and waited for an opportunity to reveal his growing affection for her. Plainly, she was the only woman in his simple life. He fought against the rising longing he had for her. If he expressed it, he suspected his days as an Indianatlantic cop would be over.

Then, one morning after a long and trying night shift, he suggested they meet for breakfast. She agreed and his spirits soared. She insisted they drive thirty minutes away to avoid being seen by other officers. She was guarded in their conversation and Nolan realized just how worried she was about losing her job. Now, a few months later, they were still dating in secret. Nolan was growing frustrated and felt that the secrecy seemed more important to her than their relationship.

"I need some backup, Stacie, and I am hoping you can help me out," he said.

"What's up?" she asked. She did not invite Nolan in. It perturbed him.

"Clara Morgan just got roughed up by the military at the checkpoint in front of the station. She was trying to report problems at the Thomas house."

"Yeah, well, that's probably one of many reports flooding in. Doesn't Morgan have us on speed dial?"

"Yeah, she does, but I promised her I would check it out," he replied. "Listen, you can stay here, I know you can't leave right away. Take this radio and I'll check in when I look at the house."

"This seems a little over-vigilant considering the source," she said.

"I know, it's better than sitting on my ass. For three days now. People need us out there and we need to be seen in the neighborhoods," he said. "I don't want to break all the rules and I can't make a call like this without some sort of backup. I also thought this radio might be one way to get around the moratorium on communication."

"Listen," she replied, "my mom is here. I can go with you. Give me a minute to get dressed."

She left the door open as she turned and he stepped into the air conditioning. There was a television going on in the background playing a kids show of some sort. Nolan pulled the door shut and waited. Five minutes turned into ten and he was just about to knock on the door when he heard Stacie talking. He heard her approach and then she came out the door with her uniform on.

"You look marvelous, dear," said Nolan trying to be funny using a British accent.

"Right-o."

They walked out into the sun and she stopped.

"You must be kidding," she said, staring at the golf cart.

"Hey, it beats being a bicycle cop," he said, "It's Clara Morgan's and when we are done I am going to take it back to her place. She's in the hospital, roughed up badly by GIs. They don't protect and defend like we do."

They climbed aboard and headed back toward Riverside. Nolan described in detail all that happened as they approached the Thomas residence.

Pulling up in front, they checked their radios. There was an intercom on the front gate and Nolan pushed the call button. Nobody answered. He waited, and then pressed it again.

"So, do we need a warrant?" he asked Raisch.

"I don't think so," she replied. "There has been a report of a murder, for all we know, somebody is hurt inside."

They walked up the sidewalk to the front door. Nolan pressed the doorbell and it rang.

"Well, the electricity is on."

"It was on back at the gate, too, Sherlock," Raisch said with a smile.

"Oh, yeah," said Nolan, "I guess it was."

They waited a few seconds. "Nothing moving," he said. Then he knocked loud and hard.

"Ben Thomas, are you okay? This is the Indianatlantic Town Police," Nolan's voice hung in the humid air.

"You know," he said after fifteen seconds, "Clara said that I should make sure to check out back. Let's go have a look."

Hands on holsters, they walked around the side of the house toward the water. Nolan stopped and looked out at the Indian River.

"That's quite a boat," he said, "I don't think that old man Thomas would sail something like that."

"No, you're right. That boat is big," she said.

"It is not just the size. That is a blue water boat."

Nolan had come to Melbourne on his alcoholic father's boat. One night the old man, half drunk and angry, fell overboard and drowned. He was found drifting in the marina. Nolan woke up the next morning to find his stoic mother downright happy over it. They sold the boat and Nolan's mother and younger brother bought a small house on Merritt Island. He had spent most of his teenage years on the big sailboat and secretly hoped to sail once again. Not in the cards.

Nolan stepped aboard for a better look. In the distance a small boat was motoring away from them. It was about halfway to the mainland. Nolan noted the missing dinghy and then looked up again.

"What?" asked Raisch.

"Probably nothing." He stepped into the large teak and brushed aluminum cockpit. He twirled in the captain's seat and fingered the console, loaded with electronics. All digital these days, not like the analog dials he grew up with. He looked into the salon through the glass entryway.

"Nobody here, all locked up."

"Good," said Raisch impatiently. "Let's get up to the house."

Nolan stopped and took out his mobile phone. He snapped a picture of the registration numbers on the bow.

Nolan looked in through the glass doors. He pressed on the glass and moved his hand. The door easily slid open.

"Not locked," he said. He put his face up to the four-inch crack. "Mr. Thomas, are you home?" he said forcefully and loudly.

Nolan pushed the door open more. Raisch stopped him with her left hand. With her right hand she unsnapped her holster. He did the same. He then stepped quickly into the kitchen, moving his weapon to the left. Raisch followed immediately after, moving hers to the right.

"Clear," he said.

"Clear," she responded.

They scanned the room in silence.

"Let's go a little further in," he said.

They walked across the kitchen, almost back to back, and came into the wide entrance leading to the living room.

"Shit, Nolan," she said as they both froze in place.

A large red blood splatter, crudely wiped but plainly visible, stood out on the opposite wall about six feet from the floor.

31

ACROSS THE RIVER

Dan turned his steps toward the Indian River to the east. Riverview Park was there and he was thinking that this would be a good staging place to ferry supplies over to the *Caruso*. North was Crane Creek and they could potentially find a spot there as well.

He walked a couple blocks off the main street now and there were homes lining old streets. Many of the Old Florida homes were small, two-bedroom bungalows that blossomed in the late 1950s and early space years of the 1960s and had the look of worn beach rentals. The street typically gave way to a sandy parking area in front. Ungainly chain link fences adorned many of them and then, in the middle of what looked rather rough, a well- tended yard, featuring palms, sabals, Washingtonians or something else. The homeowners had painstakingly planted tropical plants and the stark difference from the surrounding homes made them all that more appealing. Dan wondered who lived behind the doors and what sort of survival preparations any of them had made.

A huge, dilapidated cabin cruiser sat on one lawn ahead. Maybe 26 feet, it was propped up by railroad timber and weeds had grown up as far as the gunwales. As Dan got closer he saw a group of young men were sitting around a fire pit in the front yard. Before he was directly in front, he turned left to avoid them. One of the men called out to him.

"Hey," said a large man with a thick bushy red beard, "Where are you heading?"

Dan continued walking and acted as if he had not heard the man.

"Hey, you!" he barked again. "You live here?"

Dan kept walking. He heard hurried steps behind him. He quickly slung his backpack down in front of him and turned, his right hand sliding toward his back to clear the gun should it be needed.

"Dude!" said the man seeing Dan's defensive moves. "It's cool. We are just making sure nobody is looting."

"Just walking to the park," Dan answered. "No looting."

The group back by the fire had stopped talking and were all staring in their direction.

"What's in the park?" Red Beard asked.

"I have a boat tied up in the Indian River and I am going to take a look at her," replied Dan.

The man nodded. "Okay, we don't want any problems around here."

"Understood," said Dan, "I am going to be walking back through here after I check things out and I might be coming back with my family in tow. Maybe in the next few days. You have seen me now, and I know you. Are we good?"

Dan slowly reached into his backpack and withdrew a pack of cigarettes.

"I don't smoke, man," he said curtly, the tension rising immediately.

"Well, that's all I can offer and it's as good as cash. I am just trying to be friendly and mind my own business."

"Just because we are a bunch of rednecks doesn't mean we are going to hurt you."

"Sorry, I didn't mean any offense." Dan stashed the cigarettes.

"Alright," said the man through his large bearded face, "We're not going to have any problems around here." It was a statement of fact and Dan couldn't fault him for watching his neighborhood.

"No sir, no problems. I agree."

Dan zipped up his backpack and slung it onto his shoulder. He extended his hand and said, "Thanks. I appreciate your position here and won't make any problems. My name is Dan."

The big man gripped Dan's hand and said, "Caine. Good luck." He turned and crossed the street to rejoin his campfire friends.

Dan scanned the neighborhood. The afternoon light was beginning to fail now and the previous golden hues began to look like a low, misty cloud.

Dan reached the park. There were no vehicles parked in the lot, usually overflowing with trucks and trailers. Across the park a couple of homeless folks had pitched a dilapidated tent. Further north was an old boat ramp. It would still serve his needs, he thought, since all he had was the small Zodiac. He walked up to the edge of the water, picking his way through some mangrove and riprap. He dropped to one knee and grabbed the binoculars.

The sun was now low, almost gone. Behind him the rays shot toward the east making for excellent visibility. A light chop, maybe one to three footers on the Indian River made the water sparkle with diamonds even this late. Even fifteen minutes later it might have been impossible to see across.

He pushed the two halves of the binoculars closer together to scan the horizon. He saw a small boat motoring directly his way about halfway across the waterway. He scanned upward until he found the edge of the water. Then back on a horizontal line and...there. There she was. She looked to be in fine order. A sense of joy flooded him and he realized how worried he had been. Maybe for no reason.

Dan smiled, dropping the binoculars for a moment. He sat still and let the moment sink in. Then he lifted the binoculars again and focused on the *Caruso*. He could barely see her details. He scanned down to the dinghy once again. It was heading directly toward him and would arrive in another five minutes or so. It was best not to meet any more strangers so he stood, swung the backpack and started back.

As he walked the shoreline, he scanned for launch points. He would have to tow the small inflatable back here using the ATV and then find a good launch spot. It was too big for him to outright lift but perhaps he and Kyle could slide it down into the water. As darkness grew Dan stuck to the neighborhood streets, avoiding the main road, until he was almost parallel with the warehouse. He hugged close to the water which meant the larger, more expensive homes were on his left. He then cut west and crossed over Highway 1.

As he approached the warehouse a group of young men were loitering on the sidewalk, no less than a hundred feet from the entrance. He paused and ducked back around the side. No sense in encountering anybody he did not have to. For the first time he noted that the wind had shifted. It was too dark to see the clouds, though he knew there was a low ceiling. The weather might be turning wet. The same group was still there. He'd circle the block rather than enter under their watchful eyes. He rounded the back of the warehouse building. He keyed his radio a couple of times.

The static on his radio was broken by somebody keying their radio in a similar but slightly different pattern. He pushed the button to talk, "Rear entrance." Seconds later the reinforced metal door opened and Dan stepped into the arms of his wife. They embraced like it had been a year.

32

BLOODY MESS

Nolan checked his watch. The sun would be down soon and an hour later curfew would set in. They had to get going or they would be stuck out on the streets with the military on the loose.

"Let's go call this in," he said to Stacie. She was using her phone to capture the crime scene in its current state.

"Call it into who?" she asked.

"You mean whom," he replied.

"What?" she asked.

"You said *who* but you should have said *whom*," he replied.

"Nolan, here we are doing police work in the midst of complete societal breakdown and you are giving me grammar lessons."

"Sorry," he replied. "Let's get out of here. We need the print kit. And get Melbourne's forensic team in here."

"We had better check the rest of the house first. There could be a body or something else obvious."

He knew she was right. *She is thorough*, he thought. He admired her for that.

"I'll check the bedrooms," she said. "You go look at the garage and that boat out back." She pointed with her chin.

Nolan turned and opened the door leading into the garage. He flipped on the light switch. A Town Car. He used his phone to snap a picture of the plate and he felt the hood, which was cold. He pulled out his flashlight and peered into the backseat. Something shiny caught his attention. He took out a handkerchief and used it to shield his touch from the door handle as he opened the rear driver's side door. He saw a spent bullet casing in the crease where the bench and the seat back met. He snapped a photo with his phone but left the casing in place. He dropped to the floor and, using the flashlight, looked under the car. Nothing. He then opened the driver's door and saw a button for the trunk. He pushed it and went back to take a look at the spacious, empty trunk. He closed up the car and walked back into the house.

As he was doing this, Raisch searched two bedrooms where she saw nothing unusual. Then she entered the master bedroom. Signs of a burglary were everywhere. A couple drawers were opened and not fully shut, their contents askew. She turned on a light in the closet. An empty jewelry hanger, a jewelry box, empty and on the floor, greeted her. She saw that the closet had been ransacked and then halfway picked up. It was not well done and she wondered if the burglar had been surprised by somebody.

She met Nolan in the kitchen as he was about to head out. He was looking closely at the aluminum tracks on which the glass door slid. In the 90 degree angle there was blood. Somebody had wiped it but had not taken the time to do a good job. He pointed at it without saying anything and Raisch nodded her head.

They went out back and walked down the length of the sidewalk to the cement pier. The large, white catamaran was in stark relief against the darkening water front. The golden rays of the sun had passed below the horizon. Nolan stepped aboard and flicked his flashlight to look inside. Nothing looked out of place. Raisch tried to open the hatch leading into the boat's interior but it was locked.

"No dinghy," said Nolan. The ropes that secured the sailboat's tender to the davits swung in the breeze. The rope was cut.

"Somebody could have taken it after the murders," he offered. She shrugged.

Nolan whistled. "Twin screws. Look at that turnbuckle," he wrapped his hand around the starboard stay. "Oversized stainless steel. Lazyjacks, too," he said looking up the mast.

"Well, whatever that all means," said Raisch.

"Yeah, you're right. We gotta go. Right now," said Nolan, realizing that it was now dark.

They walked back out through the house, locking the door, knowing the sliding glass doors in the back were still open. They climbed into the golf cart and Nolan gunned the electric motor as they rolled down the street toward Raisch's place.

"What do you make of it?" he asked.

"It looks like a murder scene without a body to me."

"I'll try to call Melbourne. If they don't answer, I am going back to see if we can pull any fingerprints in the morning."

"I'll try to join you," she said.

Nolan knew that her daughter was probably home as school was canceled.

They rode in silence back to her house.

As they pulled up she turned to Nolan and said, "My ex is in town. That's why my mom is staying with me."

Raisch's ex-husband had caused her a lot of pain. She shared some of this with him and Nolan knew it. She had eventually got a restraining order against him, fearing for her life. She also worried that he would take her daughter, Kaitlynn.

"Sorry," said Nolan. "Has he come around lately?"

"Yeah, he has. He came to the door and I told him to fuck off and I thought he was going to hit me."

"Keep the radio. I will keep mine on. Just call if he comes back."

They pulled up in front of her place.

"Okay, thanks," she said, stepping out of the golf cart. "Next time you pick me up for a date, why don't you borrow your dad's car?" She smiled at him.

"Good advice," he said. "Does this mean we have officially been on our first date?"

"Slow down, slugger," she said, turning her back on him and walking up the sidewalk.

He waited until she was inside. *What did she mean by that? She didn't really mean slow down,* he wondered. *How could they go any slower?*

"What am I doing?" he whispered to himself.

He spun a circle and headed for the station. It was now dark and he looked for a switch to turn on the headlights. No headlights. He had fifteen minutes before the curfew clamped down.

As he turned the corner onto 5th Street, he slowed as he approached the checkpoint. The low whirr of the golf cart let him glide right up to the checkpoint and he stopped. Nobody had noticed him. He called out, "Hey, Police Officer Nolan approaching."

Lights, bright and blinding, enveloped him. He instinctively raised his hands off the steering wheel and squinted. A young voice off to his left tried to sound authoritative.

"Sir, you cannot come through this checkpoint."

"I am a police officer who works here, I am on duty, and I need to get to my post." Nolan spoke in a no-nonsense tone, trying to control his temper.

"I am not authorized to let anybody through, sir."

"Call your commanding officer, then."

Fifteen long minutes later, Nolan was sitting at his desk, checking to see if the phone worked. One way or another, he was going to appeal to whoever was in charge out there and get somebody working this double murder case.

33

BACK ONSHORE

Dog squinted into the failing light, searching where he could tie up the dinghy. He could run aground or wander aimlessly as the sun had dropped fast. He searched for a cigarette and did not find one. Ahead he could make out the outline of the low buildings. Did they have a dock?

He aimed the boat north just a little for Crane Creek, a small estuary rimmed first with marinas, then expensive homes and then just middle-class Florida cinder block homes. Up ahead was a small island where he had partied as a teenager. He could ditch the boat on the island and nobody would mess with it.

Should he take Jillian back to his new residence? Had the old lady seen anything? Of course she had. There was blood everywhere. Why was that front door open? Even if she had seen something, who would pay attention to her? The cops had their hands full. Nobody was stopping the looters. Why would they care about an old rich couple, half dead anyway?

He steered straight down the middle of Crane Creek. It was now dark, no streetlights and only a few homes with electricity, powered by generators, and he began to think about the curfew. How long would it take for him to get back to Jillian at her mom's place? What would happen if he rolled up and she was not there?

The island appeared in the darkness as the waterway narrowed. The sewage treatment plant announced itself from downwind to the left. He'd tie up there instead of the island. No sense swimming in the dark with a bag to carry. He had hardly stopped when a swarm of mosquitoes and no-see-ums descended. He stood back and looked at the mangrove, trying to estimate the height of the tide. Satisfied that he had given the rope enough slack but not too much, he hustled through the treatment plant swinging the canvas tote.

The dirt road gave way to a narrow paved road. He noticed that there were lights on in houses and that nobody was out. Was it curfew? As he approached busy Highway 1, he stayed a block west of it but cut back to the north, toward the bridge. As he approached the creek again he realized that the only way across was that main road. Risky.

He slowed as he got to the corner. He stopped and studied the street in both directions. A convoy of maybe a dozen armored vehicles and olive drab trucks headed toward him. He retreated against a white building, empty and abandoned. He moved around the corner and the small convoy sped past him. Brake lights lit as they slowed on the bridge. They were setting up a checkpoint.

"Damn," Dog whispered.

He had to cross that bridge or bunk down for the night on this side of the bridge. He could swim but really did not want to do that. Then he remembered the old train trestle.

Just a few hundred feet to the west an old track ran across Crane's Creek. It had been built in the late 1800s and more than one bridge walker had been killed trying to cross on a dare. A teenage Dog had himself leaped into the river when a freighter rumbled down on him.

Dog was soon carefully picking his way down the tracks. As he approached the end of the bridge, a knot of men huddled under the walkway that crossed under the railway. There was a small park and pavilion next to where they stood. Dog stepped forward.

"Who is that?" came a male voice.

Dog kept walking.

"Hey, stop. Who is that?"

Dog continued forward. Men spoke urgently. Then he heard running footsteps. He shifted the tote to his left hand and pulled out the handgun with his right.

Dog faced another hundred feet of railway in front of him before the bridge dropped to the ground. He ran as fast as he could. He was hitting every third railroad tie and doing his best to keep from busting an ankle. Damn cigarettes, he huffed.

As he cleared the track, he broke into a full sprint. Dog was big, but not fast. Two or three men were running him down and he knew that they could catch him. He slowed, stopped and turned around brandishing the gun.

He couldn't see his pursuers. They must have seen the gun. They had been there moments before. Now they were gone. Dog slowly turned in a circle. Nobody.

"Funny, guys," he shouted, "Stop fucking with me!"

Silence.

Dog slowly retreated in the direction he was hoping to go. He heard somebody scrambling. He turned around. He was hit flat in the face with a shovel. Down he went. As he fell his arm swung in an arc and he depressed the trigger. The gun barked in his hand and for a split second he saw a man spin away from the force of a bullet, the shovel flying.

Dog hit the ground and tucked his shoulder, rolling with the impact. He held the tote tight to his chest. He struggled to stop in a way that would bring the gun back up into a firing position. He saw two men backing up. They looked at Dog, they looked at their fallen friend, and held their hands up in mock surrender. They backed up a few feet and then turned to sprint off.

Dog felt his face with his left hand. Warm, moist and he tasted something salty, like iron. His nose lurched to the left in an unnatural way. He pushed on it only to feel intense pain across his face. His eye was swelling. He rolled onto his hands and knees, letting his head drop. A stream of blood flowed onto the sand from his nose.

"Shit," he said. He sat back on his calves and tilted his head back to stem the bleeding. He sat like this for minutes that seemed like hours, trying to catch his breath but breathing through his mouth.

He stood and stumbled backwards, stepping on something soft. He looked down. He had stepped on the wrist of the man he had shot. He was looking up at Dog with vacant eyes. A bullet had taken out a good piece of his neck as his blood pooled to the soil instead of his arteries. He was not moving but Dog could see the rhythm of the blood as his heart pulsed its last beats.

Dog was still clutching the tote. He searched for his gun and found it. He turned back to the dying man.

"Dumbshit," he said as he walked off in the direction of Jillian and her mother's house.

34

DOG'S NIGHT

When Jillian opened the door she put her hand over her mouth in shock.

"Dog, what happened?"

"I got jumped back by Crane Creek," he said slowly. "Need to sit down before I pass out."

Jillian would've kissed him but the blood revolted her. She guided him inside to the couch. He dropped the tote. He had been holding the gun in the other hand and eased it to the floor. He buried his bloodied head in his dirt-blackened hands.

"I am going to clean you up," she said. "You need some water."

She got a stack of towels and a bucket of water. She soaked the towel and pushed his head up until he screamed. His cheek was scraped and his nose was still bleeding. She winced, whispered and then gently wiped at his wounded face until most of the blood was gone. Bruising circled his right eye and a cut stood out across his eyebrow.

He looked at her as she worked and wondered what made her so kind and loving. He felt his heart bursting with emotions: love for her, regret for the dead man, panic for their future. He needed a drink and a smoke. Dog started to cry.

"Dog, c'mon, stop it," she said. "You are going to be okay. It looks a lot worse than it is," she lied.

"Jill, you are so good to me. I am such a loser, and you are so loving to me. Too damn good."

She smiled but said nothing.

"Jill, I got the bastard."

"Well, I think he got you, too," she replied.

"No, I mean I got him."

She was silent, not disapproving and not approving as she continued to dab his face.

"I need a drink," he said. He reached for the tote and withdrew the vodka. Only a puddle remained, which he dispatched quickly.

"Lay down," she said, guiding him down on the couch and then elevating his feet. He did not fit on the couch and this was the only way for him to lay flat.

"Jill, I got a plan for us." She unwrapped the bandage on his arm. He winced and swore.

"Yeah?" she said. "What's the plan?"

He wanted to tell her in detail but thought better of it. He grimaced as she pulled off the last bit stuck to his wound.

"I think you should come with me tomorrow and I will show you."

"I can't stay here," she said. He noted a change in her voice. "Nobody will come and take Mom away."

He was just about to suggest she call around for help when she continued.

"I called everybody I can think of. In another day it is going to be a real problem. A crisis. I need to get away from here. I made my peace. There is nothing I can do now."

Dog grunted his agreement. She bawled.

"I hate this. No food, the electricity comes and goes. The air conditioning is off half the day. I can't walk outside without feeling like I am going to be beaten up. And Mom. I can't leave her but I have to."

Her sobbing grew as she dropped her head down on Dog's chest.

He was warm, hairy, salty and reassuring. He stroked her hair, caressed her breasts.

"Tomorrow you are going to come with me. I got us a boat, Jill. A big boat. A boat big enough to sail away from here for good."

She cried more, her chest heaving into him.

"Tomorrow we are going, Jill. There is nothing to be sad about. You were good to your mom. Now it's time for us to get the hell out of here."

"Dog, how? We have no money. Even on a boat you need money."

He lifted the tote and turned it over. Gold coins, necklaces and rings poured out onto the floor. She knew he had to have stolen it. She looked at him and then back at the carpet. He assumed her judgment and he was right to.

"Don't worry about it, Jill. They were old people who were already dead. I took it after they were dead. They weren't going to need it. Tomorrow I will show you. There is nobody left in the house and they don't need the boat. We can just go sail it out of here tomorrow."

"Okay, Dog. If that is what you are doing, I am doing it, too."

She climbed out of his embrace and went into the kitchen, returning with some aspirin and a glass of water. He took the aspirin and drained the glass.

"Now I need some real medicine," he said.

"You sit back now," she said, "You're going to be sore in the morning. There is no booze left here."

A moment of panic flooded over him. He thought about getting up and going to see what he might find in town. Then, common sense took hold. He fell back on the couch.

In a few minutes he was asleep.

She got up and took the towels to the kitchen. She sat at the kitchen table, lit a cigarette, and took a long drag.

He came back. She was surprised but grateful. It had been a day and a half and in that time, she could get no one out to pick up her mother's body. It lay in the next room. Jillian had decided that she could do nothing about it. She had walked to Smith's Funeral Home and found it locked up. She had walked to the Indianatlantic police station to find sentries who told her to report it to a hospital. She called the hospital and they took down her name and number. They would call back, they had said, but nobody had. Then her phone quit working. When it connected again she could not get through to the hospital. The whole day was a dead end.

When Dog had left she was glad. Now she was glad he was back.

"What is wrong with me?" she asked herself. She finished her cigarette, then moved to the couch and leaned back on Dog's shoulder. She was soon fast asleep despite the loud and rumbling snores from Dog's twisted nose and mouth.

35

NOLAN'S NIGHT

Officer Nolan heard a door open down the hall. He stood and went out and saw Gerald Mains, the chief of the Indianatlantic Police, pause at the reception desk.

"Hey," said Nolan.

Mains looked up and saw Nolan.

"You still here?" asked Mains.

"Well, of course. I was asked to stay back," Nolan replied.

"That was a couple days ago. I didn't think you would be here the whole time."

"I was out a bit," Nolan replied, "There was a call that I had to attend to. Other than that, though, I have been here."

"For Christ's sake, Nolan. Nobody expected you to stay here the whole two days."

Nolan's temper flared for a moment and then he checked himself.

"I was asked to stay, so I stayed."

"I am here now, so you should go home and get some sleep," said Mains.

Nolan wanted to say, "You're welcome," or "Of course I did my duty as instructed," or even, "I was here while you were sitting on your fat ass at home." Instead, he held his tongue.

"Curfew is on," said Nolan, "It's too dangerous to go out now."

"Aw shit, Nolan. I just walked over and didn't see a living thing until I got right up by the station. There is a little guard post out there but the kid soldiers didn't say a word to me."

Home to his empty apartment? The thought depressed him.

"I'm going to bunk in my office tonight," he replied.

"Suit yourself," said the chief as he walked in the opposite direction toward his office.

"I am going to shower up so don't shoot me if you hear me walking around."

The chief just shrugged and continued on.

A half hour later, as Nolan stirred a cup of instant ramen, he sat down on his couch wearing gym shorts and a t-shirt from his locker. He ate and then leaned back on the couch, drawing a thin blanket over himself.

He could not sleep. He thought about Stacie and wondered if she was up right now. He thought about the big catamaran. He wondered who owned it. He weighed just how much he hated his job. If Mains had shown him just a little gratitude, he might feel differently. He tried hard and considered himself a good cop. Then he thought about the rest of the officers and that led him back to Stacie. Was it time for him to force the issue with her? Was it too soon?

He awoke with a jerk. The radio had cackled to life inches from his head. It was garbled. He pressed the transmit button, "Come again?"

There was silence and then a voice said, "Unit 4, is that you?" Unit 4 was the Nolan/Raisch team.

"Yeah, it's me," said Nolan, forgoing police talk.

"I need to get out of here," Raisch replied.

"What?" asked Nolan.

"I need to get out of here with my daughter," she replied.

Nolan was confused, then asked, "What do you mean?"

"My ex is back and I need to get out of here, dammit."

"Okay, settle down. Let me see if I can get a car and come over. Be in touch shortly."

Nolan walked down the hall in his gym shorts and bare feet. Even after three days in the station it felt strange. He saw a light on in the chief's office. He walked down and tapped on the closed door.

"Yeah, come in."

Chief Mains sprawled behind his desk.

"I just got a call on this radio from somebody who needs some help. I'd like to take a car and go check it out."

"Nolan, you were just pissing your pants about the curfew and now you want a car?" He shook his head with a disgusted look. "No. You can't have a car. None of us can. Got it? Not at night. Go back to bed and worry about it in the morning."

Nolan shuffled back to his office. He slowly dressed in his civilian clothes, thinking through his next steps. A plan was forming in his head. It was now, or never. Sometimes events conspired for something great to happen.

He stuck his wallet in his back pocket and clipped his keys to a belt loop. He grabbed his service revolver, the radio and a flashlight. He clipped the radio on his jeans. No throat plate, no vest and no blue uniform. He felt very strange. Naked even. He picked up his badge and looked at it. He threw it in the trash can next to his desk. Then he thought better of it and picked it up.

He quietly let himself out into the humid Florida evening. He walked over to Clara's golf cart and silently sped off through the parking lot avoiding the checkpoint. About ten minutes later he pulled up in front of Raisch's place. He keyed the radio once and paused. Then again and whispered, "Out front." He walked to the front door just as Raisch opened it.

He looked at her face and anger rose from deep within him. Her eye was black and a purple cut streaked the side of her temple. She had a laceration on her neck and it was bruising.

"He hit you?"

"Yeah," she said sullenly. "That bastard likes to hit me."

"Jesus, Stacie, why didn't you just shoot him?"

"I am a single mom, Nolan. I can't afford to lose the only job I love. If I shot him, I would be off of the force and you know it. I would never work as a cop again."

"I will shoot him then."

"Phillip," she said using his first name for the first time in their relationship, "You are a good man and a good cop. You don't want to get messed up in this. He is trouble. I am trouble. Save yourself before it's too late."

"I already am mixed up in it. And I am glad I am, Stacie. Can I come in?"

Thirty minutes later she stared at him. They were sitting at her kitchen table. He leaned in toward her and said, "But we gotta go now. Or we don't go at all."

"Nolan, I should say Phillip, are you sure about this?"

"As sure as I have been about anything in my life," he responded.

"It's not just me, it's Kaitlynn. This is a big commitment, Nolan."

"You can officially call me Phil from now on," he said. "Look, you are vulnerable, I know that. I am not going to take advantage of you. I think we should be together, but you decide that for yourself when you are good and ready. Now we have an option we are not going to have in twenty-four hours."

Raisch thought about it. This would be a gamble like none she had ever made. What about her daughter? If Kaitlynn's father came back, and he swore he would, the twisted relationship would most likely end in bloodshed. She looked into Nolan's eyes.

"We're cops," she said factually. "We have a situation here."

Nolan gathered his thoughts before speaking. "We haven't been cops for the past few days and I don't think this mess is going to fix itself anytime soon. Keep the big picture in mind."

She was silent. She gripped his hand in both of hers. Then she asked, "So, Phil, how long can a person live on a boat that big anyway?"

36

DAN'S NIGHT

Dan had undressed in the office, showered and was toweling dry when Kate handed him a beer. They clinked their bottles together in a mock toast. They sat down on either side of the desk Dan had picked up from a garbage pile down the street months before.

"Thanks, dear."

"Thanks goes to you for keeping the fridge here stocked," she said.

"Yeah, but other than beer, there must not be much."

"No, but that's okay," she said. "We had a good night around here. We made some microwave popcorn and played a few games before they went to bed."

He drank deeply, feeling some satisfaction.

"Well, our boat is still there and I learned a lot. Sounds like the feds are working fast to restore order. They've taken over the food distribution system and restocking the big stores. They are also controlling the gas stations. The panic caught them off guard, but they are responding to it now."

"Are we leaving too early?"

"No, babe, we most definitely are not leaving too early."

"Was it safe out there?"

"I ran into a neighborhood watch group. I thought they might be a problem but they weren't. Other than that, I didn't have any trouble. A lot of looting, though, and so people are starting to fight back."

"What else?"

"I stopped at a bar and a truck driver told me some stuff. He had been driving supplies under the direction of the military. Big cities in Florida are lawless. Tampa, Orlando, Miami. Jacksonville sounds like the worst. Here in Melbourne things are pretty calm compared to those places."

"What caused this mess? The attacks in Asia had nothing to do with us."

"Society is thin, Kate. There are three days of reserves in our stores at most. All of this emphasis on just-in-time inventory means that our infrastructure has to run smoothly. Credit, the movement of money, gas, roads, all of it. If any of those pieces gets into trouble, the integrated system collapses. Blockchain breaks."

"Are we in for a nuclear winter?"

"I think so, but nobody really knows because the world has never been on the brink of chaos like this before."

"Dan, you've killed two people and Cooper has killed one man. What is going to happen when the law catches up to us?"

Dan squirmed in the canvas chair, crossed his legs, rubbed his sunburned arms. He looked into Kate's eyes.

"Self defense at worst, Kate. But there was no law out there. I heard at the bar that a militia was trying to control the area between here and Orlando. We talked about this and we knew that it was possible. It has come to pass."

"Talking about it when life was..." she paused looking for the right word, "...Solid is very different now that we are shooting people."

"Kate. We made the decision to survive. In a crisis like this people will take advantage of others. I don't mean just rob and loot. People are evil. You know that."

She was silent. Without looking up, she said, "I thought we were the good guys."

"We are the good guys," he responded forcefully, frustration evident.

"Keep your voice down. It doesn't feel like we are very good right now."

He sat back in his seat and glanced at his watch.

"Kate, what would it take for you to feel that we are doing the right thing?"

"We could start by not killing people."

"Dammit!" He stood and walked around the back of the chair.

"Think for a minute. What were those two guys back at the river going to do next? Tell me."

She shook her head having nothing to say.

"I will tell you, then. They were going to kill our boys, rape you and then find Sophie and do who knows what to her. What is it that you can't see about that situation? We had no choice. I had no choice. Even your fourteen-year-old son knew who the bad guys were."

Tears welled up as she stared down at the table.

"Kate, we didn't ask for this. But we knew it might come to this."

"Dan, listen, I understand what you are saying is factually correct. But that doesn't make it easy and that doesn't make it morally right. What good does it do us to survive if we become people that we don't want to be?"

He was angry. He tried to calm himself. His emotions turned from frustration to empathy.

"I am sorry Kate. You're right. We need to survive but we also need to keep our humanity intact. What you did with that soldier is who you are. You save lives. I love you for that and I don't want you to lose that part of who you are."

She gave up a muted smile and looked up into his eyes. He was confused. What was the right thing to say?

"What can we do to make sure that we keep our humanity?"

She peeled the label off her beer bottle. "We help people we can along the way."

Dan nodded in agreement.

"You did that this morning, Kate."

"We pray, read the Bible and keep our faith intact."

"Sure," he said, "we can do that."

"Dan, I want you to do that. Not just me. This has to be you too."

The biggest tension in their marriage had been her insistence on attending church as a family. Dan participated, but she had always felt that she pushed him in a direction he did not want to go.

"Sure. It's my intention to do this anyway. I might need some help in remembering."

"Our kids need to see us love each other, Dan. We have to keep our marriage intact."

He reached across the table and took hold of her hands in his.

"That's what I want too."

"Maybe we should go and consummate this marriage again," she said with a provocative smile.

Dan was amazed by his wife.

"When was the last time we did it in a sleeping bag?" he asked in a whisper.

"I don't know. But this is also a part of our humanity."

37

WEATHER

At 2 am a thunderous explosion shook the seaside city of Melbourne. It started as a low rumble and then another explosion shook the ground. Six jolts in all thundered through town until things fell silent.

Dan sat up, panicked. He got up, went down to the rear door, unlocked it and slowly opened it. A dusty red glow in the sky to the west appeared in the general direction they had come from the night before. He began to hear some shouting in the distance as people crept out in the night to investigate. He locked the door.

Climbing back into his zippered sleeping bag, Kate asked, "Sonic booms?"

"No, I don't think so. I think they dropped some ordnance on Deseret Ranch."

"Bombs?"

"Could be missiles, a drone. Dunno, dear."

He tried to get back to sleep but his mind was stirring. Lists of supplies, extra things to add, the route they would take to the waterfront.

The biggest question he had to solve was about the number of trips they must make. If he had been better prepared, they could do it in one trip with the whole family. As it stood, he needed at least two supply runs first. He couldn't leave the ATV at the park. Was it too exposed there? What were his alternatives? His mind churned for over an hour until exhaustion took over.

At 5:45 his eyes popped open. He was not certain of the time but sure enough to know that it was morning. He had to get up either way. His bladder was begging for relief. He pulled out his notepad and walked up as quietly as he could to the upper room. He started a new set of lists. Instead of topical, such as "Sailing Gear," and "Food Stores," this list was based on containers. Container A held most of the tools and equipment. Container B, which was added later, had more survival gear, food and personal items. In the last weeks, though, they had gotten mixed up. He'd get Kyle and Cooper busy as soon as they woke.

He went back upstairs. As he turned he saw Cooper sitting at the little table on a folding chair.

"Hey buddy," Dan whispered. "Are you ready for our adventure at sea?"

"Yeah," he quietly offered. He fell silent for a moment.

"Dad, am I going to get arrested for shooting that man?"

"No, Cooper. It was self-defense. You were only protecting yourself and our family."

"Kyle said the police will arrest us if they find us."

"Kyle is wrong about that. Listen, with everything going on right now, lots of dangerous people are around. Nobody wanted trouble and we knew that others were being hurt. You did what any reasonable person would do."

"Kyle said he would never shoot anybody."

Dan simmered a little below the surface. Surely Kyle knew better than to say something like that to Cooper, given the circumstances.

"Coop, we've had this talk before, only we had it when most of this wasn't real. We agreed that taking a life was the very last resort. We would only shoot to save our own lives or to save the lives of others. That is what happened out there. People are scared and they are acting in strange and wild ways they would not act if things were normal. Those criminals would hurt us, probably kill us, and not think twice about it. They would hurt others, too. You should not feel guilty about what happened."

Dan could see Cooper's head nodding in the dim light. Dan stood next to his son and put his free hand on his shoulder, hugging him lightly.

"I am scared, Dad."

"Everybody is scared, Coop. Those men were acting out of their fear, too. We need to make sure that we never let our fear turn us into evil people, though. That's what happened to them."

"They didn't seem to be afraid."

"Well, they are. Everybody struggles with fear."

"Are you afraid, Dad?"

"Yeah, a little. But we have each other and we have already decided that we will ride this thing out. We made plans. Now we just have to get out on the boat and stay at sea for a while."

"Kyle says we can never come back."

Dan wanted to throttle Kyle.

"We don't know what the future holds. But we'll do whatever we can to make sure we are safe. It's probably best that we accept that things will never be the same again."

"Like what?"

"Well, our home, my job, your school. These things are different now. We can't go back now and when we do, they will be different. That is really part of life, Cooper. It's just that now there is a lot of change coming at us all at once. Some people will never make the shift to what is new. They will have a hard time."

"But we will do it, right?"

"That's right, little man."

Kate came up the steps. She stopped at the top and Dan could see her outline.

"What are you two talking about?"

"We were talking about getting out on that boat today," declared Dan in as positive a way as he could.

"Today is the big day, isn't it?" she asked.

"Yes, I'm trying to figure out how we will get across with all this stuff," Dan said. "I wish we had another boat."

"Can you get one?" she asked.

"Thought about trying."

Just then a strong wind picked up outside. "Better check the weather radio right now," Dan said. A few seconds later he was coming up the stairs and Kate could hear the dull monotone computer-generated voice of the NOAA weather warning system. Dan set the radio down in the middle of the table. He turned it up.

* WINDS...SOUTHWEST WINDS WILL INCREASE TO 10 TO 20 KNOTS WITH

FREQUENT GUSTS TO 25 KNOTS TONIGHT AND CONTINUE THROUGH SATURDAY

MORNING. THE WINDS WILL THEN SHIFT TO NORTH-WEST AND INCREASE

THROUGH SATURDAY AFTERNOON. NORTHWEST WINDS 15 TO 25 KNOTS WITH

FREQUENT GUSTS BETWEEN 35 AND 40 KNOTS WILL DEVELOP LATE

SATURDAY AFTERNOON AND CONTINUE INTO SUNDAY EVENING. THE WINDS

WILL BEGIN TO DIMINISH LATE SUNDAY NIGHT.

* SEAS...SHORT-PERIOD AND STEEP HAZARDOUS SEAS BETWEEN 10 AND 12

FEET WILL DEVELOP SATURDAY AFTERNOON...THEN BUILD TO BETWEEN 15

AND 20 FEET SATURDAY NIGHT INTO SUNDAY. SHORT-PERIOD WAVES WILL

DEVELOP IN THE INTERCOASTAL WATERWAY. EXPECT WAVES TO REACH A

HEIGHT OF 4 TO 5 FEET.

. . .

PRECAUTIONARY/PREPAREDNESS ACTIONS...

A GALE WARNING MEANS WINDS OF 34 TO 47 KNOTS ARE IMMINENT OR
    OCCURRING. OPERATING A VESSEL IN GALE CONDITIONS REQUIRES
    EXPERIENCE AND PROPERLY EQUIPPED VESSELS. IT IS HIGHLY
    RECOMMENDED   THAT   MARINERS   WITHOUT   THE PROPER EXPERIENCE SEEK SAFE
    HARBOR PRIOR TO THE ONSET OF GALE CONDITIONS.
    INEXPERIENCED MARINERS...ESPECIALLY THOSE OPER-ATING SMALLER
    VESSELS   SHOULD   AVOID   NAVIGATING   IN   THESE CONDITIONS.

THE RADIO DRONED ON and Dan waited until he heard the tide report. Then he clicked off the radio.

"That ain't good," he said.

"We had better get moving."

38

FIRST RUN

Dan's plan had been to make three or four trips with gear. They'd ferry over supplies first and then ride over together in the final trip. He had to rethink this plan. The Zodiac was stable for a small boat and unsinkable. It was a great boat given the windy conditions, but he could no longer count on Kyle or Cooper taking a trip without him.

He realized that he would have to launch the boat and return the ATV, walk back and then go over. On the return trip he would be motoring in a dangerous following sea, with the wind at his back.

They would leave more supplies behind. He concluded that they would have to figure out a way to come back in a few weeks or months. Hopefully, no looters would break into the warehouse stash by then. He sipped coffee and looked up to see Kate in the doorway.

"We are going over this morning, after one supply run."

She didn't say anything, but he knew what she was thinking.

"We can't wait anymore, dear. We don't know what will happen here in Melbourne. Things could settle down or things might get terrible."

Kate had a fear of big seas. She had been extremely seasick occasionally and knew the danger of the phrase "gale force winds."

She finally spoke. "We should wait."

He shook his head no and looked at her.

"If we could, we would. We can't take that chance."

Kate turned and walked away. He pushed his wife into situations that were difficult for her. But this was different. In his mind, it was now or never. He planned the arguments he could use on her. Her fear was real. She had good reason to be afraid. She also was a little irrational because of the past few days of crisis.

He found her leaning against the office wall, her face in her hands crying. He took her in his arms in a bear hug. "Babe, let me make one trip over with supplies and then we will decide. Does that sound fair?"

She shook her head yes and buried her head in his shoulder. He held her, and they stood for three or four minutes until her sobbing ceased. Kyle walked by, heading up the stairs, and as he went he said, "Get a room."

Dan looked up at him and smiled. Then he said, "You and I will have a talk, buddy." Kyle shrugged in return and leaped up the stairs.

An hour later, the Zodiac's trailer was hooked up to the ATV. Dan jumped onto the seat and he nodded to Kate.

He keyed his radio and there was a bark of feedback from two other radios. She pulled the long chain on the bay door and it crunched open. Dan started forward, Kyle walking alongside him. Besides the handgun on his hip, an AR-15 rifle stood straight up and down, its muzzle stuck in a piece of PVC piping that Dan had tied to the ATV frame. People would see the gun from a distance, and that is what he wanted.

Dan drove out onto Highway 1 and pointed it north. He was afraid of overheating the ATV with the very full boat, so he crawled along. Kyle followed right behind, a rifle slung over his shoulder. There was nothing subtle about their plan. They looked armed and dangerous to strangers. They'd skip the exposed beach at the park. He would go down Highway 1 and find a spot to put into Crane Creek, which was much more protected. It was between tides, so there would be minimal current.

Fifteen minutes later, crawling along at snail's pace, they had yet to see a single moving car. Nobody was out. Dan crossed the road and drove down an embankment toward a parking lot near the water and very accessible. Dan could see the old railway bridge just down Crane Creek. As he circled to back up the boat, the first wave of rain hit them.

He walked to the back of the Zodiac and squeezed the black gas bulb until it was hard. Kyle looked at him with a question about what was to happen next. Dan handed him the boat keys.

"Go under the bridge here and tie off to a piling right in the middle. If somebody comes up, move off so that you keep a good distance. I'll be back in twenty minutes. You stay put."

Dan unhooked the trailer winch.

"If I am more than, say, an hour, anchor off in the middle of the river and swim over and walk back to the warehouse. Keep your rifle on you and do your best to avoid people."

"Yeah, sure," said Kyle, with a hint of impatience.

Dan froze and looked him in the eye. "Don't play around here. Got it?"

Kyle nodded and climbed up into the Zodiac. Dan put the ATV in reverse and slowly backed up. The boat would not float off the trailer at first, but eventually, it came free. The motor leapt to life and Dan saw Kyle move backwards in the water, turn around and head toward the middle of channel. Dan fastened the winch strap, turned around, and took off at high speed for the warehouse. He couldn't waste daylight.

39

NOLAN

Nolan was so filled with excitement that he hadn't slept all night.

After leaving Raisch's house, he was tempted to head straight to the boat and check it out. But it was night, and there was a curfew. He also knew that between now and the morning not much would change. He returned to his lonely apartment.

As he struggled to come off a bad night of sleep, he turned on his computer. He had a bank account with plenty of cash in it, but he couldn't get it. Just the same, he thought he would check it only to find that the internet was down.

He took a shower, wondering how long the water would be working. The electricity as well. Standing in his underwear, he looked into his empty refrigerator. He went back to his bedroom and pulled out a duffel bag. He filled it with clothing, extra shoes, and his toiletries. He was restless. He realized he did not have a plan for himself or his partner. He sat down on his couch to think.

He did not know whose boat it was. No way it belonged to the old man. Somebody had put a lot of pride and effort into that boat. He thought about the need to get it ready for sea. It looked prepared, but he needed a punch list, to check the engines and do a lot of prep work including a float plan. He heard the wind outside and got up to open his blinds just as a sheet of windy rain speckled the concrete slab. Well, bad weather. No big deal for him.

He was not in a hurry. He would take today to get the boat ready and then tomorrow he would lead Stacie onto their new floating getaway. That meant he probably had to check in over at the station in the morning to keep any suspicion out of the picture and then he would spend the afternoon onboard. He would check everything out and then visit Stacie.

They would need food right away. He'd put on his police uniform and go down to the grocery. He knew there were some issues with distribution but surely a cop could get his hands on a shopping cart or two of food. He would check in with Stacie on his way.

He got up to dress. He looked at the polyester uniform in a special part of his closet. His chest badge and flat badge were displayed on a small table. He always lined them up, facing up, ready for action. A feeling of sadness and guilt overtook him. He stepped in the pants and slipped the short-sleeved shirt on. He took the heavy gear belt off the hook in the closet and strapped it on. No Kevlar vest today. That was a waste of time, anyway. He opened the drawer and withdrew his Glock. He opened it and checked the chamber, letting it slip shut, just like he had done almost every workday for the past few years.

Dammit, was he going to cry? What was wrong with him? He loved that uniform and he was about to betray it. His anger got the better of him, and his resolve returned. He was a good cop. He went above and beyond, and for that he got ridiculed by his superiors. He slipped on his hat.

"Fuck 'em," he said out loud. He never swore. It did not feel right coming from his mouth.

He shuffled out the front door of the townhouse and immediately turned around and went back in for his large, oversized rain poncho. He felt in the pocket and withdrew a clear plastic cover for his hat, slipping it into place. He lifted the garage door. Clara's golf cart was pushed up to one side, barely fitting next to his nine-year-old Honda Accord.

He parked the cart at the rear of the station and noticed the rise in wind. The back door was locked and the code did not work. He walked around to the front of the building and saw the MPs milling about in the same place as before. He paid no attention and, dressed in his police poncho, walked through the lobby and back toward his desk.

He punched the space bar on his computer, and amazingly the screen lit up. He put in his code while extracting his mobile phone from his pants pocket. He opened up the boat registry and tapped in the bow numbers.

Dan Littrel, 10144 Hidden Dunes Lane, Orlando, FL 32832

Nolan used his mouse to highlight the name and address. He flipped over to the police database and pasted in the name and address. A picture and history of Dan Littrel filled the screen. The image was about two years old and used for his license renewal.

The history was unremarkable. The address was a little over four years old. No arrests, not even a traffic ticket. *It would be easier,* Nolan thought to himself, *if the guy had been a lawyer or politician.* Dan Littrel had a permit to carry a concealed weapon. *Well,* mused Nolan, *he is not a man given to violence, based on his record.*

"Watcha doing?" came a voice from his open doorway. Nolan jumped.

"Geez, Mains, you scared the crap out of me," retorted Nolan.

"What are you doing? You look guilty as hell."

"Nothing, nothing. Just going through some of my files." As he said this, he looked up at Mains while trying to close the windows on his computer.

"Well, Nolan, since you are here and you are the only cop on duty besides me, I have a job for you. I have to stay here, so you get to be the first on site. Somebody on North Riverside just let the Army MPs know that a dead body is floating in the Intercoastal. Go check it out."

Mains tossed a sheet of paper on Nolan's desk.

"Take a car. There is no backup, so don't be stupid." Mains turned and walked out.

"Okay," Nolan replied, his voice raising to project down the hall, "I need about 10 minutes to finish up here."

Nolan thought: *A car will be helpful.* Plenty of time before he was due back to pick up Stacie. They would wait until late afternoon and try to take the boat out. His mind wandered for a moment. *What if she backs out? She won't.* In any case, he had time to kill. He would go look and make a report.

He printed Dan's profile. He opened up a word processing document and made a list of all the gear they would need for the initial days of the voyage. He regretted not having an inventory of the sailboat's lockers. He went online and searched and typed in a query, "sailboat provisioning." He got a page of results, found one a little more simple and printed it.

He did another query, "differences catamaran monohull" and pressed Enter. He scanned the page. What the heck, he thought, and printed a copy. He stuffed all the copies into a clear plastic file folder and then sealed the top.

He stood and looked around. *This could be the last time he would see this little place,* he thought. His life as an Indianatlantic Police Officer would be over. He stood and went out to the lobby to find a key to the squad car. For the last damn time.

40

JILLIAN AND DOG

Dog woke up, and the day was well along. His head hurt like nothing he had ever felt before. The light streaming between the cheap plastic shutters make him clap his hand over his eyes. *Whoa,* he thought, *my eyes.* One side of his face was swollen and the stretched skin felt strange, as if it was not a part of him. He pressed slightly and a sharper pain greeted him. His hand slid down his face and he found scrapes and hardened scabs. He tried to sit up, and his entire body revolted.

I need a drink, he thought to himself. *Whatever I can get.* He sat up slowly for a second time and his feet hit the floor. He tried to open his eyes a little wider and found his left eye refusing to open at all.

"Jillian!" A second later she was there.

"Oh Dog, I am so sorry. Oh my God!" she said as she took his face in her soft hands. "I'll clean you up."

Two minutes later she was once again cleaning up dried blood. He held a bag of ice wrapped in a towel on his face as she worked.

"We're leaving today," he declared. "It's fucking dangerous out there."

"Okay." She knew that it was useless to argue and she wanted out.

"Do you have anything to drink?"

"Hang on, let me get you some water," she replied, immediately stepping away.

He had meant some alcohol but water was good right now.

"Take these," she offered and he scooped the aspirin up, tossing them into his mouth and then gulping the full glass down.

"What do you have for food?"

"I could make pancakes," she offered.

"You dumb bitch," his impatience growing. "I mean to take to sea with us. On the damn boat."

"I'll look," she said flatly, turning stoic under his rebuke.

"Aw, babe, I am sorry." He knew right away he overreacted.

"It's fine," she said, even more stoic. "Let me see what we have."

"Just put it all in a bag we can carry."

She left him as he stood and inched to the bathroom. He stumbled back into the kitchen where Jillian was emptying the meager shelves into a black garbage bag. She handed him a box.

"I found this in the cupboard."

He held it up, uncertain about what to do with it.

"It's wine in a box." She rolled her eyes at him. "Give it back."

Thirty seconds later, he was downing a tall glass of white wine.

He left the kitchen and found the treasure tote. He scooped up the contents and went back into the bedroom, got dressed and retrieved the gun.

Back in the kitchen, Jillian was pulling on a cigarette and guzzling wine. She had been crying and Dog immediately went on the defensive.

"I am sorry," he said, before knowing what it was he had done.

"I am walking out on my dead momma," she said through tears.

When Dog realized her crying was not his fault, his spirits lifted. For once, he was not to blame.

"C'mon now, Jill, that's not your mom anymore. Why don't you go pack your bag and let's get the hell out of here."

She looked up at him and half smiled while crying. *Women can be so crazy,* Dog thought. He kept his mouth shut.

"How long am I packing for?" she asked, her smile even bigger.

He smiled back. "Forever." She hugged him, he squeezed her butt and then she went to pack.

Thirty minutes later they were walking toward the sewage treatment plant. Dog had the tote over one shoulder and held the black plastic garbage bag with the other. Jillian was pulling a rolling suitcase. It was large, and she was straining to pull it, but Dog did not seem to notice. The wind was humming at a good clip and a sheet or two of rain had already darkened the road. The smell of wet asphalt, humid and stifling, along with ozone filled the air.

They soon cleared the pavement and the cement sidewalk. Dog finally stopped to turn around and glare at Jillian who could no longer keep up with the huge case. She withered under his stare but continued to struggle forward.

"Alright," he said curtly after watching her. "Give me the damn thing."

"Here, let me carry something else," she offered, grabbing for the tote.

"Hell no," he replied sharply, "that's our future in that bag."

He handed her the large plastic bag, straining to contain its contents. He mumbled a curse under his breath and grabbed the handle. He lifted it effortlessly and stomped off. Jillian could barely keep up. He stopped to make some adjustments. The handgun dug into his belly where he had stuffed it into his pants. He transferred it into the tote. He shifted his load from one side of his body to the other.

Dog walked up to the woods. He stopped and turned to wait for Jillian to catch up. The rain was still riding in on bands of wind. She reached him and he motioned for her to stay put, took the tote and pulled the gun from under his shirt. He scouted toward the river.

He came back a minute later, motioning her forward. She pushed her hair back and rubbed at the mosquitoes and no-see-ums that were already alighting on her cheek and forehead and she was soon climbing into the rubber boat. Dog threw the suitcase into the dinghy and then carefully placed the tote on the seat. He unlashed the lines and pushed out as hard as he could. The little boat broke free as Dog tumbled up and over the gunwale.

He wiped the rain from his right eye and turned the key. Nothing happened. He tried again. Nothing.

"What the fuck?" he yelled into wind. It was taking them further inland and pressing them to cross the creek.

He looked for the battery in the stern. There he found nothing but the empty battery box.

The two battery leads dangled, cut clean with a tool. Dog whipped around toward the bow in anger.

"I have to start it with the pull cord!" he screamed at her uncomprehending face.

He turned back, grasped the black handle on the top of the engine and yanked with all of his strength. To his horror, the braided rope snapped in his hand and the remaining cord recoiled into the engine.

"Damn!" he screamed into the gathering storm. He turned toward Jillian and threw the black handle at her. She cowered for cover in the bow. She could find none.

DAN BUZZED through the neighborhood as fast as he could on the ATV. Too fast and he might get stopped, not fast enough and Kyle might have problems on his own. He sensed the darkening storm over his shoulder and realized that the wind was picking up to maybe 15 mph. As he came up to Highway 1, he slowed for vehicles on the road ahead. He strained to see as much as he could without drawing attention to himself.

He clicked the button on the radio a couple times. A reassuring click pattern came back. Dan adjusted the radio to go up a couple frequencies.

"Be there in a minute," he said quietly but clearly.

"Open the door now?"

Dan hesitated while he moved forward. "Yes, now, please."

As he rounded the corner, the door was going up. He was unhappy to see about half a dozen people in a group, standing on the sidewalk in front of the warehouse. There was a car in the road as well, but Dan could not slow down to look. He turned a tight corner and said, "Slam it down."

Kate did so. He looked over at his wife and saw that she was holding an AR-15 at waist height. He chuckled, proud of her for being ready. He turned off the ATV. He wanted to say, "You can't shoot accurately holding it like that," but wisdom got the upper hand. He simply nodded his approval.

Sophie came over and hugged his leg, preventing him from getting off the bike.

"Hey, Soph," said Dan as he ran his fingers through his hair, "Great to see y'all. I am afraid I have to take off, though."

He looked up at Kate.

"Everything is fine. Kyle has the Zodiac and is waiting for me."

"Taking your backpack?" She asked as he walked toward the rear door.

"Nope, this is gray man time."

"Gray man?" she asked.

"The gray man doesn't stick out." Dan said. "Sometimes we carry rifles and look scary. Sometimes we act scared, like everybody else. Sometimes, we just try to not draw attention. Now it's time for the latter."

She shook her head as if to say, "Oh brother," as her husband stuffed the radio under his shirt.

"It is about to storm really bad. In ten minutes, those people won't be hanging out in the street. We'll be fine. The Zodiac is made for bad weather." He kissed her on the cheek and unlocked the back door. As soon as he stepped outside, the door barricade clanged back into place.

The first drops of rain came as Dan purposefully ambled down Highway 1. Within a few minutes the rain was coming down in torrents. Nobody was on the road, and Dan was ready to be wet. It beat the ghastly Florida heat of the previous few days.

Dan reached Crane Creek uneventfully. Kyle was tied up under the bridge, in between the pilings. He whistled and saw Kyle spring to life, motor buzzing. Dan stepped onto the boat and shoved off hard. A wind was pushing them.

"Let me take her," he yelled to Kyle.

Dan turned the nose into the wind. Here inside the mouth of the creek he would have no trouble, but once they popped out into the river the waves would grow to maybe a 2 to 3 foot chop. Nothing like the ocean, of course, but enough so he had to pay attention.

Dan wiped the spray from the boat compass and eyeballed his current heading. The storm was approaching from the southwest. If he kept the nose heading into the wind, their forward progress would be slow but steady. The boat was riding low. It would be sluggish, but he had a sense of confidence that comes from waterfront experience. As he approached the mouth of Crane Creek, it dawned on him that the rain was cold, not warm. Most tropical storms brought warm air up from the south. If the clouds were tall, then the moisture might fall from a great height. This could mean hail.

As they cleared the creek mouth, the wind and waves picked up. It was still late morning and he could not see across the river. He double-checked his bearings. There was no bilge pump, no battery or other extra equipment. Now he was simply glad to have the tiller in hand so he could feel the reassuring vibration of the outboard.

The little boat chugged forward. Dan figured less than 4 or 5 knots, but that would be fine so long as they kept moving forward. The wind halted for just a second and he saw the bridge off to his left. Perfect, he said to himself, just keep going. He pulled out his GPS unit and looked up the waypoint he had set for the *Caruso*.

He worried about taking the family back through this. On the up side, nobody would be stopping them to check IDs. On the down side, they were still on the front end of this disturbance. Gale force winds at sea? Nothing could be done but ride it out. Poor Kate.

Kyle was sitting with his back to the wind, doing his best to stay as dry as possible. He glanced up at Dan and gave him a thumbs up. *Always up for adventure* Dan thought as he smiled back at Kyle.

Over the next twenty minutes the motor had started a rhythm of sorts, churning loudly as the prop rose too high out of the water, and cavitated only to be shoved back down when the waves dropped them. Visibility was maybe 30-40 feet. Going too slow, however, affected his steering more than he liked.

Then, as if an iceberg, the shape of the *Caruso* came into focus. The waves subdued as they approached the lee shoreline and Kyle took a length of dock rope in hand. He looked back at his dad. "We will tie her up in the dinghy's place." Kyle nodded, and they maneuvered into position. He captured the cleat on the deck on the first attempt and pulled the boat in taut. Dan cleated another rope from the other side of the deck. They pulled again, and both tied off.

Dan stepped aboard the *Caruso*. The feeling of being home overwhelmed him, and he gave Kyle a hard slap on the back.

"Good job, son. We are almost there."

41

DOG FIGURES IT OUT

Dog looked at the tannic creek. He was sodden, sore and lacked the physical strength to jump up and dive in. His head hurt. He froze. Jillian looked on as the little boat was being pushed out into the creek. In a minute they would be across to the other side, or pushed back toward the island. Would they tangle in the mangroves or just drift downstream? She was afraid to say anything.

Dog's anger bubbled up from deep within. *Damn it,* he said to himself, *why has everything got to be so hard? Who stole that battery? Why did they have to find the boat? They could have just stolen it. Then they would not be adrift in the middle of the creek. Why would such a little boat have a goddamn battery, anyway?* He could hardly come up with curse words fast enough to satisfy his raging anger.

And then he remembered.

Dog suddenly turned in his seat. He pushed the tiller hard to the right and reached around the back of the boat motor. He unclipped the cowling and grabbed it with two hands, lifting it up and back at the same time. He turned it over and set it on his lap. He reached in and pulled out a short coiled rope with a handle. He looked up at Jillian with a smile.

"See? The emergency pull cord." She had no idea what he was talking about yet relieved by his sudden calm.

"They always put an emergency start cord inside these motors," he said in triumph.

He turned back to the motor and wound the little cord around a groove on the top of the engine. He stopped to prime the gas bulb. He studied the tiller handle for a moment and set it to start. Then, with an enormous tug, he pulled the rope. The motor sputtered for a second, and he immediately twisted the handle. The engine stopped.

He shook his head but started to wrap the cord around the flywheel again. He squeezed the bulb for good measure. He reset the position of the throttle on the tiller handle. Jillian leaned forward to avoid getting scraped by the black mangroves along the bank of the island. The rain struck them hard. He pulled the cord. He grabbed the tiller handle, but this time didn't twist it.

The engine caught and hummed in a cloud of blue smoke. He waited about three seconds and then slowly turned the handle. They swung around in the stream. "Hot damn! We are on our way!" he smiled at her. She smiled back, relieved as much by the fact of being on the way as by Dog's mood.

He set the tiller on a slow speed while he wrestled the cowling back into place. He snapped the lid shut and throttled the little boat up to its highest speed. Jillian fell back and scrambled to recover her balance.

"Sorry," he laughed through the sound of the wind and rain.

They approached the railway trestle over the creek.

"That's where I got set up last night!" he yelled over the motor and weather. He pointed off to the north. "Fuckers!"

Jillian looked north. No visibility. She turned to Dog with a loud voice and asked, "Are you sure we're safe out there in this little thing?"

"Yeah." She was not as certain as he was.

As they approached the creek's mouth, the wave action picked up and sloshed over the bow. The boat bounced. Jillian sat rigid on the front bench, holding herself down. Dog kept the boat at full-throttle making the situation uncomfortable for him and downright frightening for her. After a few minutes, he experimented by slowing down. The boat stopped slapping and they pressed forward.

A torrent of wind descended on them. A wave hit them head on and Jillian was tossed to the deck for a second time. She scrambled back up. She turned to give Dog a dirty look. The rear bench empty, no Dog in sight.

"Oh, no!" she screamed into the wind. "Oh, no!" She shook with fear. She cried and screamed "no," all the while the little boat motored in circles. Then she crawled to the rear seat. She had only watched others command a boat. She gripped two hands on the tiller and pushed it. The boat immediately swerved. She pushed it further, going in a semicircle. The whole time she cried and moaned, "No, no, Dog, where the hell are you?"

Despite the waves, she could still see a small line of bubbles riding the water roughly where they had just been. She tried to follow the bubble line. She screamed out, "Dog!" and then paused. Then again, and again. She sobbed and tried to scream again.

Just as she opened her mouth, she heard him. "Jillian!" It was him! She cried again and half stood, only to be knocked back down on the bench.

"Jillian!" He was close but where? Then between the waves she saw his head bob. She slid right past him, not knowing how to slow down the motor and the boat.

"I see you!" She turned the handle toward him and came straight at him. He swam to the port side and, just as she passed, he screamed, "Twist the handle!"

She looked down at the tiller. She twisted it and the little motor roared louder. She understood. She turned it the other way, and it slowed. Dog swam toward her as best he could. He grabbed the edge of the rubber boat, but there was nothing to hang onto.

She panicked. She looked for a way to help. The emergency pull cord sat in bilge water at the bottom of the boat. She ran it under the bench and handed the two ends to him. He clung on.

"Go back," he said, "I can't get in now." She could barely see the mainland but it was there. She twisted the handle and sped up just a little, making sure that he was okay.

"I am so sorry, Dog." She was still crying.

"You did good, Jill. Really good." His voice was weak and hoarse. "Just too tired to get in."

The thin cord bit into his hands, but he was too weak and scared to readjust his grip. He tried to lift his arms up higher to hang on as best he could.

She drove the little boat straight up the shoreline. She came in where there were no rocks or mangroves, just a slope of sand. Luckily, the propeller hit bottom with a thud, and the motor stopped. Dog stood on wary legs and hobbled around the back of the boat. Waves beat it further ashore. He unlocked the motor's tilt and lifted the propeller at its top position. He half pushed, half tried to keep up as the boat pushed further ashore. Soon it could go no further and he sat down on the rubbery gunwale, tossing the emergency pull cord into the boat.

JILLIAN LOOKED AT HIM. He was bruised, scraped and defeated. He had been shot, punched, kicked and now this. His head hung down on his heaving chest as he gulped air. She stepped out and came around to where he perched. She wrapped her arms around him and laid her head on his shoulder.

"I love you, Dog. Don't ever do that again."

He took her hand and pressed his cheek softly against her wet hair and heaving bosom.

"I won't. Jill. I love you, too."

42

BACK TO THE MAINLAND

Dan dug into this pocket and withdrew a set of keys. He walked through the cockpit and unlocked the sliding glass door leading into the salon. Kyle had hefted bundles up onto the slightly rolling deck then stowed gear below on the deck between the starboard staterooms.

As Kyle got to work, Dan used cockpit electronics to check the freshwater levels and battery levels. The solar panels had kept the batteries topped off. The water in the holding tanks would be fine for months. He checked that off his mental to-do list. He turned on the radio and hit the button for the emergency weather channel. The report was monotonously the same and he turned it off. Kyle appeared by his side.

"All done," he said.

"Can you go unwrap the rifles in case they got wet? You know where to put them."

"Yep," and he disappeared again.

Dan looked up at the house. He should let Ben know they were heading out, bad weather or not. He knew the old man would want to talk him out of it. It was hard to have a short conversation with Ben. Dan felt guilty, but he also had a return trip to make. The weather would only get worse. He had a higher priority right now. Dan replaced the blue canvas cockpit covers. He spun around to see Kyle coming back up. Dan shut and locked the salon door. He pushed the keys deep into his pocket.

"Let's go. It might be harder to get back than it was to get here."

They boarded the Zodiac and each tossed off a rope.

He would have to check on Ben when they returned.

The wind continued to whip and within one hundred feet of the lee shore, the whitecaps were already roiling. Dan tried to match the boat speed to the wave period, but it was impossible. He was glad it was late morning. There was plenty of daylight. By the time they got back to the warehouse, they could eat then all walk back to the Zodiac together.

The part that worried Dan the most was leaving the boat tied up in the creek. His options were limited. He could ask Kyle to wait with the boat while he got the ATV. Kyle could wait until they all returned. Or, they could just tie it up under the bridge. None of these options were good. He put off deciding for now, but he knew that with the wind at their back, this would be a very short trip.

"Dad!" Kyle's call pulled Dan back to reality. "Check it out."

The wind continued, the waves did not change but a break in the cloud cover revealed a blue streak of sky. The tropical storm bands separated, creating a stark beauty. Dan knew this was simply a break in the cloud cover, but it felt good to see the blue sky. For the past weeks, it had been nothing but a dusty copper color interspersed with gray overtones.

They rode the waves back toward the mouth of the creek. As soon as the break came, it left and a sheet of rain covered them up.

Dan continued to play out the day, estimating time and wondering if they could sail out tonight with the storm growing. Kate would oppose that plan.

He wondered about Patrick Air Force Base. When they sailed south toward Sebastian Inlet, they would be under its watchful eyes. Manned sentries, drones, radar and who knows what else, like motion detectors. Was that good or bad? Leaving at night would help, but probably not possibly in the shallow waters of the Indian River. He thought about the tide. Storm surge would mute the outbound tide at the Inlet.

He felt that the whole situation was conspiring against him. He awoke that morning, intent on sleeping at sea. Now it didn't seem possible. He felt his spirits drop a notch. He was failing his family and himself.

The course of action seemed clear now. Kyle would wait with the boat. Dan would get the ATV and the trailer home. If they had to stay in the warehouse another night, this was the safest plan all around. He had known this all along, just had to convince himself.

"Kyle, you wait in the boat while I get the ATV."

Kyle looked at Dan and was quiet for a moment. Then he said, "You giving up on today?"

"Not yet, but probably. I have a feeling we'll stay in the warehouse."

As they entered Crane Creek, the waves turned more manageable. They pulled up to the south shoreline and Dan stepped out. He pushed Kyle back out and said, "Tie off but if anybody approaches, be ready to cast off and avoid them."

"Nobody's going to be out here, Dad. See you in a few."

Dan turned toward the warehouse. No one in sight. Waves of rain and wind continued to cross in front of him and he began to jog. Nobody was at the warehouse this time. He keyed his radio and waited. Then he keyed it again. Kate's voice came on.

"Go around back. It's too windy."

He stepped into the dry warehouse.

"I'm going back for Kyle with the ATV," he said quickly, "and I don't want to waste any time."

"Okay, what do you need me to do?"

"Nothing. Get the door for me. Back in a few."

Twenty minutes later Dan repeated the radio procedure. He pulled in and Kyle stepped in right behind him. The door slid shut.

Dan shut off the ATV and stood to stretch. Sophie looked at him with a little smile.

"You are wet," she said.

"It's raining outside. Cats and dogs." He smiled back at her.

Soon Dan was dry and sipping hot coffee. The weather radio on the table continued to drone bad news about the deteriorating situation.

"It's going to be worse in the morning. I think we should take off now." He was trying to convince himself as much as he was trying to convince Kate.

She pursed her lips. Dan could read the *no* coming before she said it. But he was wrong. She looked into his eyes and said, "If you think it's best to go now, then let's get moving."

From somewhere back in the warehouse, a 14-year-old boy said, "It's about time!"

43

DEAD BODY

Nolan stepped outside into a strong wind. He thought about the timing of this storm. Hurricane season was a few months off and this felt like a serious storm. A no-name storm? Could this be the nuclear situation messing with the weather? He dismissed the idea as he walked to the squad car.

He got in. The air conditioner felt good even at this hour and with the rain. He waited for the laptop computer to boot up. He picked up the microphone to let dispatch know he was heading out, but then stopped. There was nobody at the dispatch desk. He withdrew the paper from his breast pocket and looked at the address on the report. He immediately knew the house. A few doors down from the Thomas place. He backed up.

He was tempted to see Raisch. This body had to be Ben Thomas floating in the water. Did he want to call attention to the murder now? What if they sent over forensics and the team hung out at the house all day? He would simply treat it like the report it was and go look. The log time on the report was now almost forty minutes ago. That was plenty of time for the body to wash back out to sea in this wind.

He pulled up in front of a house behind a brick fence just north of the Thomas home. He braced for the windy, wet blast. He stuffed the report back into his pocket, grabbed his rain poncho and a pair of binoculars. He stepped out into the rain.

The large house in front of him had the look of successful businessman all over it. He went through the gate and up to the front door. He punched the doorbell. Seconds later, it opened and a short, balding man in cargo shorts and a Hawaiian shirt stared back at him.

"You thought you would show up, eh?" the man said as he extracted a cigar from between clenched teeth. "I called you almost an hour ago."

"Sorry sir, I came as soon as possible. Can I come in?"

"Yeah, yeah, c'mon, get out of the rain."

"Thanks, and your name would be?" Nolan asked, leaving the question hanging in expectation of an answer.

"Kroft. Wayne Kroft. My wife went down to move the Adirondack chairs back because of the wind. She came back to the house screaming. A body floating in the water. I told her she was full of shit, of course, until I looked and she was right." Kroft used his cigar to punctuate his points, getting closer to Nolan's face with each jab.

"Do you want to show me?"

"Sure. Hang on, let me get a jacket. Come on, walk through here." Kroft pointed the way toward the back of the house.

Nolan walked through a huge open living room and kitchen area. There were windows all across the back, and the view was million-dollar impressive. They exited out the sliding door and moved through the rain toward the cement slab that crossed the entire lot, backing onto the water. A 50-foot Donzi speed boat was hoisted up on a boat lift toward the right and a set of walk out steps dropped to sea level.

"It was just here up against the seawall." Kroft leaned to peer into the water.

Nolan did likewise and scanned the area. Nothing there.

"Dammit, it was there."

"Did you take a cell phone picture?" asked Nolan.

"The damn mobile phone isn't working half the time," replied

Kroft with an angry edge to his voice. "I am telling you it was right here."

Nolan was scanning further out on every side.

"Let's both of us just look for a moment, Mr. Kroft. It might be here somewhere close by."

Nolan lifted his binoculars and scanned from left to right in a pattern, going further out with each pass. As he made his third pass, he saw something lifted by a wave. He kept scanning and said nothing to Kroft. The intensity of the rain picked up and Kroft muttered an oath. Nolan scanned back to the spot and focused the binoculars. Something big was bobbing in the waves. Nolan knew it was the body, although ID would be impossible until he found a medical examiner. Good luck with that.. He let the binoculars drop, holding them with one hand.

"Let's go inside," said Nolan as he turned, "It's getting worse."

They hurried inside.

"Is your wife here?" Nolan asked Kroft.

Without warning, Kroft bellowed out "Lorraine" and Nolan jumped.

"Sorry," said Kroft.

"It's okay," replied Nolan, "Are you certain you saw a body?"

"Hell yeah it was a body," he replied, "We could see the back, the gray head and the arms out to the side."

"There is no chance it was a large fish, dolphin or something?" Nolan probed.

"No, dammit, we aren't crazy old people."

Lorraine entered the room and said, "It was a body, Officer."

"Was it clothed?" asked Nolan.

"Yes, it was," said Lorraine, "And I think it was a man because it was big and the hair was from a man."

"Okay, well, we will make a report and I want you to keep checking when the weather gets better. Without something further, there isn't much we can do about it now."

Kroft rolled his eyes at Lorraine and said, "Thank you, Officer, for jack shit."

Lorraine aimed a glare at her husband. It was a look that she had evidently used before as he rolled his eyes again.

"If you see anything like that again, take a picture with your phone."

A few minutes later, Nolan was standing at Raisch's door. He had parked his car a few streets over and walked, fearful that the location of the car might be tracked. He rang the doorbell and stood back, protected by the rain in the door's alcove.

Raisch opened the door and without being asked, Nolan stepped in.

He leaned over to give her a kiss, and she obliged. It was the sort of kiss that made Nolan wonder about her motivation. Was it out of obligation or affection?

"We need to move out tonight," he stated.

"Why? I might need a little more time."

"We don't have time. A neighbor saw a body floating in the Intercoastal, just a few doors down from the Thomas house."

"And," she paused thinking. "Do you think it's from the Thomas house?"

"For sure it is," he replied, "where else might it come from?"

"Are they retrieving the body now?" "No. I went to check out the report, but the body had floated back out. I saw it with my binoculars out there, I think, but we can't wait. If it is Ben Thomas, that whole property will be off limits for a few days. We have to go tonight."

Raisch furrowed her eyebrows in thought as Nolan waited for her reply.

"This is a one way decision," she observed.

"I'm all in," he countered. "I've already decided."

She lowered her head and looked down before saying, "I am not deciding just for me, you know."

"I get it. I really do. But staying here is not much of a life for Kaitlynn, anyway."

There was a long awkward pause and Nolan was about to lay down an ultimatum when she said, "Fine. Tonight's the night."

44

BACK ACROSS

Dog lay flat on the sandy shore with his eyes closed against the wind and the rain. Grains of sand pelted the face, hands and most every sensitive patch of their uncovered skin. Jillian pressed against him for warmth and, well, love. A fatigue held him in check. The options before him were grim and scary. Staying was not possible. The little boat scared him. He wondered if Jillian would even try it with him. He nodded asleep, but then sat up as if he'd been hit with a cattle prod. He was shaking a little but was not sure if it was the tiredness or if he just needed a drink. He remembered the liquor cabinet across the water.

"We are going to walk across the damn bridge, Jill."

She looked up at him and replied, "Sure, okay, whatever you think is best." Inwardly she leapt for joy as the apprehension of the boat ride disappeared. She sat up as he did and smiled at him.

"Let me get some stuff out of the boat and let's go." A flash of lightning to the south toward Sebastian and Vero lit the beach as Dog splashed into the edge of the waves toward the boat. He returned a few moments later, the tote with all their treasures over his shoulder. Jillian stood and linked her arm in his as they walked away from the beach.

They had come ashore just south of the park. They walked up onto the dead end of a residential street and continued west, away from the water and toward A1A. As they reached the first cross street the door of the house opened with a loud squeak. It was on the southeast corner which they had just passed by. A large man stepped onto the stoop. He wore camos and a head bandana with a rifle held at his waist.

"Hold on!" he shouted out, "What the hell you doing here?"

Dog and Jillian stopped and turned toward him. Dog's hand went to his waistband for his gun and he realized it was not there. "Shit," he said under his breath.

"Stop moving, asshole!" yelled the man with the rifle. "Drop the bag. Let me see your hands."

Dog hesitated for a moment. A shot rang out from the rifle. Jillian jumped, and Dog glanced at her, thinking she had been hit.

"That's a warning shot," the man called out as he walked toward them, "Show those hands."

Both Dog and Jillian opened their hands palm out and slowly raised them.

As the man slowed down about five yards away from them Dog asked, "What the fuck, man, we're just walking on the damn street."

"Yeah, that's what looters say all the time."

"We ain't lootin' nothing," replied Dog.

"Maybe you ain't," came the reply, "Let's see what's in that bag there and we'll probably know. Kick it over here."

Dog stood still, not sure what to do. Out of the corner of his eye he saw another man approaching from his right. He had a bushy red beard and was even larger than Dog. Maybe six foot, four.

"What's up here, Sam?" he asked as he strode confidently toward them.

"I got a couple of looters here," said Sam.

Caine circled around them and stood next to Sam.

"What makes you think they're looters?"

"He's a pretty big dude and somebody has put a beatin' on him. Let's see what's in the bag of yours, big man."

The bag was hanging from Dog's left shoulder. He kept his left hand open, palm forward, while slowly moving his right hand toward the bag.

"Be cool, man," said Dog, "I'll show you what's in here."

The tote opened up and Dog slowly moved his right hand back toward it.

"Just drop the damn bag!" came an angry voice from behind the rifle.

"Be cool," said Dog, "I can't drop it. You'll know why in a second."

Curiosity got the best of Caine and he said quietly, "Just give him time."

Dog's hand slowly went down the mouth of the tote. He felt the handle of the CZ but grabbed a piece of jewelry. He didn't even know what he had, but he slowly extracted it from the bag. He held it up and tossed it. It landed between Caine and the other man. Caine stooped to pick it and held it up, examining it.

The man with the rifle said, "See, a damn looter."

"Sure looks like it," agreed Caine.

"Let me show you something else."

He once again slowly moved his right hand toward the tote.

"You'll like this." Dog's voice was smooth, and he had a slight smile on his face.

"I'm shooting that bastard."

"Let's just wait one second here," said Caine, "let's see what he's got."

Dog's hand wrapped itself around the handle of the CZ inside the tote. He feigned concern as if he were fishing around in the bag for just the right thing. He twisted his wrist in an arc, pointing the weapon at the two men. He pulled the trigger.

The bag erupted in a blast, jewelry scattering as Dog shot and simultaneously lifted the gun out of the bag. The man holding the rifle let the barrel travel upward. He pulled the trigger but to no effect. Dog's handgun was now pointed squarely at the two men. The rifle barrel was lowering back into firing position when Dog's finger jabbed another round off. This time, the bullet met its mark. It hit the rifleman in the right elbow and traveled into his chest, puncturing his lung and exiting through his back. Another wild shot blew out the end of the rifle as the man fell backward. Dog slid the sights over. Caine pivoted to run. He stumbled and fell flat on the pavement, sprawled out and placed his hands over his head.

Dog stepped forward with the gun pointed at Caine. He stood over him and Caine pleaded, "Dude, c'mon, nobody was going to shoot."

"Jill, get over here," ordered Dog.

She was weeping a few feet back from Dog. She slowly walked up to stand beside him.

"Have you ever shot somebody, Jill?"

She said nothing through the tears.

Caine slowly turned over the ground, his hands up until he was looking back at Dog towering over him.

"Have you ever fucking shot somebody, Jill?"

"No," she whispered. "Let's just go."

The gun bucked in Dog's hand. A bullet shattered Caine's throat.

Jillian snapped around to look away.

"He would have shot us in a second, without even thinking about it."

Her anguished crying rose and fell in waves of sobbing.

"Shut up, Jill."

Dog knelt to collect a few things that exploded out of the bottom of the tote. He put them back into the tote and tucked it under his arm. He started walking away, toward the bridge.

Jillian, now on her knees, watched him walk away. Between her sobs she said, "No, no," and held herself with her arms. As he got further away, she stood and hurried after him.

The rain poured again. Was she free to go? She didn't know, but she ran to catch up to him.

45

FAMILY ACROSS

Dan picked up Kyle without incident and returned to the warehouse, hauling the boat behind the ATV. He had handed out assignments to Cooper and Kyle, got Kate going on last-minute items and returned to the safety of his checklists.

There was a list of provisions, mechanical items to check, clothing and survival items, electrical items and navigational points to consider. He had been planning for months and now it was time to act. Kyle leaned in through the doorway.

"Come on, Dad, let's get going."

Kyle was right. He'd done the prep work, now it was time to execute.

"Everything loaded up?"

"Yeah, we did it all."

Dan swept the items from the desktop into a plastic bin. He had already unloaded the desk drawers into it.

"Put this into storage, Kyle."

Kyle took the bin and went outside of the office. Dan stood and felt a nervous excitement sweep over him. They were really going to do it.

He walked out into the open area of the warehouse and locked up first one, then the other container. He grabbed a pail of tools. Inside was a handheld propane torch, a pair of dark safety goggles, a stick of brazing material and a lighter. He soon had both doors welded shut. It would not stop somebody with similar equipment, but it would stop anybody who happened by without it. "Okay, let's roll." The family filed out on the trek toward the creek. Fifteen minutes later the boat slid off the trailer into the water.

Dan knew the semi-rigid inflatable boat was the best boat in the waves they were to face. Yet he worried.

He looked at Kate. "Everybody get in. I'll drive back to the warehouse while you hang out in the creek. If anybody comes along, I want you to head out without me. I'll get over to you. We can't afford anybody taking too much of an interest in us now."

She said nothing in return. Dan read the deep concern on her face.

"Yeah, I know, this is not what we want, but we might be back here if something goes wrong over there. We need the trailer and ATV until we are out at sea."

She nodded and waded out, holding Sophie, setting her on the inflated gunwale, and then jumped in. Cooper scrambled in as Kyle shoved off. A minute later they were motoring out.

Dan jumped on the ATV, gunned the engine, and started down Highway 1. The wind was picking up as a wall of rain swept in his direction. He passed a couple walking the opposite way but nobody else was out.

Dan secured the ATV and trailer and jogged through the monsoon back to his family. Sophie hailed him with a wave, so he figured all was well. They cleared the creek, certainly over the boat weight limit, but they could cross the waterway.

Dan suddenly swerved the boat back toward land.

"Check it out!" he yelled over the wind. He pointed just south of the creek's mouth. A small boat lodged up on the sandy beach.

Kate looked at him quizzically.

"The ship tender was gone. That might be it," he yelled over the whine of the motor.

Five minutes later Dan jumped over into waist deep water. It was, indeed, the ship tender from the *Caruso*. He took a line with him and attached it to the bow of the boat. It was washed up about three feet in the sand. He and Kyle shoved until it broke free. What was a suitcase and a large black plastic garbage bag doing in their vessel? He heaved them toward shore. The suitcase dropped and sank, but the bag floated. They motored off again, now with a boat in tow.

Dan hugged the bridge and steered the Zodiac into each wave and varied the speed to climb the larger waves. This rough inside, Dan wondered what the ocean might be like right now, out past the peninsula, but that was a worry for later.

About halfway across they could easily make out the *Caruso*. Ben Thomas' house loomed up behind it and, for the first time in a week, Kate felt a sense of relief.

They motored right up to the quay and Dan lashed the boat onto a cleat. They pulled the boat in tight while Kate, Cooper and Sophie climbed aboard their *Caruso*. Cooper and Kyle helped their father pull the dinghy over toward the *Caruso* and lashed it to the davits.

Kate was already inside the Caruso and Dan could see her turning on lights and talking to Sophie, who was dancing around the salon and singing. Kate filled with a sense of home. It was familiar. On the table was a scarf that she had used some weeks ago when they were out on the water. She picked it up and pressed it against her cheek. She felt the wonderful day they had spent together as a family.

Kyle and Dan emptied the contents of the Zodiac onto the quay and then carried everything onto the big catamaran.

The house was dark and he couldn't see any lights. He thought about walking up to see Ben, but he needed to comfort his family in the first semblance of a home they had in weeks. Besides, he thought, *it looks like there is a party going on inside and I don't want to miss out on that.*

46

NOLAN DECIDES

Nolan stood in the grocery checkout line for twenty minutes when he decided it wasn't worth it. There had been about fifty people in line ahead of him, but it had hardly moved. At home, his mood improved a bit when he changed into civilian clothes, and decided to make a quick trip for supplies. He needed a few tools to break into the boat, and a couple days of food since he was not sure what was on board already. And some sturdy clothes to wear aboard. Upon his arrival at the largest retail store in the area, his first warning about more trouble was the sign that read, Regional Distribution Center.

He was driving a police car but was in civilian clothes. He parked across the street and walked over in the rain. He had to provide identification to enter the store guarded by MPs. Then he was confronted with the reality of food lines. He had thought himself unusual and alone for venturing out in a tropical storm. Now he was aware of the reality that citizens were facing. Hundreds of them. The line wrapped back and forth like a security line at the Orlando airport. The shelves in the store were mostly empty. In the main aisle stood boxes that were evidently pre-packed with rationed food. People were picking up a box and moving toward the cash registers. No money was changing hands. People were presenting identification which was being typed into the cash registers by more military personnel.

He walked out.

He drove back home and ransacked the meager stocks in his apartment. Was it best to go back to the boat and see what provisions might be on board already? He grabbed a beer and sat down on the sofa. He did not want to tell Stacie about his failure to get enough food for the first few days. He did not want to go back to the house without her. It was a murder site and his police training told him it was not safe. He had every right to go back to the scene of a crime. But, he could not possibly call in to the dispatcher which is what standard procedure asked for. He stared into the empty living room and tried to sort out his options. None of them good.

He suited up in his police uniform and loaded a few boxes, some clothes and a backpack with personal papers and photos. He headed toward Ben Thomas' house.

As he approached the crime scene, he slowed. There was a couple walking up the sidewalk toward the house. The bulky man was twice the size of the timid woman who struggled to match his stride. His clothing was soiled and torn. She murmured and he answered, "Shut the hell up."

Nolan rolled the fogged window down. The man's face was bloodied, more black than blue. They froze at the sight of the cruiser. Would innocent people react that way, Nolan wondered.

His bad guy radar, honed over years of service, screamed danger.

Nolan continued his slow drive by and passed the Thomas house. Seconds later he passed the couple, and he rolled down his window. They were soaking wet, and it appeared the big man had more than one injury.

Nolan passed by them and watched them in his rearview mirror as he slowed further. He took his foot off the accelerator and was careful not to flash the brake lights. The couple turned and disappeared into the shrubs and shadows.

"Shit!" Nolan said out loud. He was certain they had turned into the Thomas residence. He punched the gas and turned the cruiser around, driving up on somebody's yard as he did so. He made another pass toward the house and once again rolled down his window. Nobody was there. They must have gone inside. He remembered that the door wasn't locked.

He pulled the cruiser over and punched the steering wheel. If he went to get Stacie and tell her what was happening, she would probably abandon their plan. He wanted her so bad. If he went back to the Thomas residence, there would be trouble. Did he want his future to be more of the past? How much of a risk was he willing to take? These people were almost certainly not supposed to be there. They might not be the killers. But he had to assume they were.

"Shit!" he yelled again, punching the steering wheel. Lightning struck somewhere close by and wind buffeted the Police Interceptor.

He picked up his cell phone. Should he call Stacie? He was always asking for input, always following the rules. Damn it, he thought to himself, he worked for a police department in the middle of an elderly retirement community. He was a pussy. He had finally made a plan, a bold plan, and now he could feel it slipping through his fingers.

"That's it," he said aloud. "Damn it all to hell."

He slammed the car in gear and swung it around. He drove until he was a block away from the house. He unlatched his seat belt. He checked his duty belt for ammo, pulled out his Glock and racked it, placing a bullet in the chamber. He adjusted his vest, which always rode high when he was driving. He grabbed the Mossberg 590M from its mount. He held it over the passenger seat and racked it once. He double-checked the chamber. Habit told him to pick up the microphone before exiting the car. A habit that felt right to break at the moment.

He opened the door and stepped out with his left foot. As soon as it hit the pavement he froze in place. He had no plan. He picked his foot up again and shut the car door. The cruiser was still running.

He spoke into the empty car again. "What am I doing?"

He was not asking himself if he would act. He had made that decision. He needed a plan. He considered the crime scene and the people in it. He thought about how to get to the front door without attracting attention. He wondered about the neighbors. He plotted how he would get into the house, and what he would do once he got there. He shut off the car and pushed the button to open the trunk. He got out, taking the keys with him, and got the large yellow Police poncho out of the trunk. He slipped it on, leaving his left arm inside. He held the Mossberg with his left hand under the poncho. He was going in the front door after knocking, like a cop on a call.

This was his time. He'd grab life by the balls and give it a jerk.

IN THE HOUSE

D og entered the house through the unlocked front door, pushing his way past Jillian and beelined for the liquor cabinet. He found the first bottle that resembled whiskey and unscrewed the top, taking a big swig. He was shaking, and he knew it was most likely from alcohol deprivation. Jillian shook her head.

"What are you going to do out in the big ocean with nothing to drink?" He took the bottle out of his mouth and said, "Fuck you," smiled, and gulped again. The warmth in his stomach would soon dull the pain in his head. She looked around the house. *Wow*, she thought, she had never been in a place like this unless she was on the cleaning team. She walked into the kitchen and opened the refrigerator. A handgun sat on the top shelf. She looked for something quick to eat and found a bag of mini-carrots not yet mushy. She grabbed it and went back to find Dog. He had sat down in a big easy chair in the living room and was removing his sodden shoes.

"Now what?" she asked.

"We wait for the storm to finish up and then we sail out of here."

For the first time she seriously thought about the sailboat. She had hardly recovered from the scare of seeing Dog overboard just a few hours before.

"Can you really drive that boat?"

"Sail it. You don't drive a sailboat. You sail it."

"Can you really sail that boat?"

"Of course I can sail it."

"You fell out of the last boat." As she said this, she tried to smile to soften the words.

He said nothing. He took another pull on the bottle.

Their conversation was interrupted by three sharp knocks on the door.

"Damn it," said Dog in a whisper, bolting upright.

Jillian stood looking at him, her face showing fear.

"Stay away from the door," he commanded.

He rose and slowly shuffled barefoot toward the entryway. He eased around the corner and felt for the Remington 870. Right where he had left it. Jillian had followed him silently.

The doorbell rang.

"Okay, Jill," Dog whispered. "Open the door and stand back. Let them come in here."

"What are you going to do?" She glared at him while whispering accusingly.

"I'm gonna kill the fucker, what do you think I am going to do?" he snapped.

She whispered back with anger, "You are not killing anybody."

Dog lifted the shotgun and turned the stock toward Jillian. He jabbed her in the face. She stumbled back in shock.

"Open the damn door, Jillian."

She put her hands up to her face, and they came away bloody. As if in a trance, she took the few steps toward the door just as the knob turned and the door slowly pushed inward. The knob met her hand, and for an instant she stopped its motion. She looked up and saw Officer Nolan's face in the crack. He was smiling at her and had begun to say something. She did not hear him. She pulled the door open and Nolan stepped inside. Concern spread on his face as he saw the blood running down her left cheek.

Nolan turned toward Dog whose large frame was standing about six feet to his left. The cop immediately recognized the barrel of a shotgun and instinctively pulled the Mossberg up with his left hand. It rose a few inches when Dog pulled the trigger on his weapon.

Nolan took the full force of the shotgun blast to his face and neck. He did not stumble. He fell backwards, first hitting the half-open door and then falling out onto the door stoop. Dog pumped his shotgun before Nolan had reached the ground. He trained the gun on the policeman's body and stepped forward. When he was satisfied that Nolan would no longer be any trouble, he grabbed Nolan's ankle. He dragged the body into the house. He kicked the door, still barefooted, he remembered too late and pain shot up his leg.

Turning around, Dog looked at Jillian. She slumped on her feet, her face was buried in her hands. She was weeping and could not talk.

Dog tried to think of something to say. All he could come up with was, "That fucker shouldn't have been here." He retreated to the bottle of liquor and took another deep drink.

Dog sank into the chair for a few minutes and wished away the fatigue of all that had happened. *That stupid cop*, he thought, *why did that bastard have to show up now?* Jillian's crying had devolved to taking deep gulps of air interspersed with sobs. He got up and limped toward her.

"Jill, c'mon, let's get you in bed. You need to rest."

"Fuck you, Dog!" she screamed.

"Knock it off, damn it," he roared, "You need to sleep this off."

"Are you going to hit me if I don't?" she screamed again.

Dog rolled his eyes. This is why he hated women. He reached down and took her by the right arm. She tried to hit him but only flailed as he pulled her down the hallway to the master bedroom. He tossed her onto the bed.

"Rest up," he said, shutting the door.

She rolled up into a ball, holding her knees against her chest and cried. *Who would die next,* she wondered.

48

ON BOARD THE CARUSO

Dan could feel his excitement rising but it was accompanied by a nervous concern that he would not be adequately prepared. He had set out his lists on the chart table. He was going through his standard pre-voyage checklist with Cooper sitting beside him, watching him intently.

"Coop, can you go check the water tanks and tell me what the level is?"

"Yes sir," said Cooper seriously, standing and turning toward the set of controls on the far wall.

Dan returned his attention to the checklists. He could hear Kate at work below, talking with Kyle and making sure that provisions were secured so they would not slide around the boat.

"Daddy," Sophie's voice broke in on his thoughts, "can we go see Mr. Ben now?"

Dan smiled at Sophie. "Not now, Soph, I gotta get some of this work done. Then we'll visit."

"Okay, Daddy," she replied. "Can I help?"

"Yeah, you can help. How about you get me a big glass of water?"

"Okay, Daddy."

Cooper came back. "Tanks are full." Dan had known, but had asked Cooper anyway.

"Okay, thanks Coop. Can you go help your mom?"

The door leading outside opened and closed. Dan felt the wind rushing in on his back. The moist, wet air filled the cabin, and he thought about how much they would miss air conditioning. Living aboard was all about controlling dampness, mildew and all the downside of a tropical Florida home afloat. He turned back to his lists. Why was he even doing this again? He knew the boat, and he knew every screw, piece of gear and box of food on the boat. The tanks were full, the ship-to-shore charging had topped up the batteries and the solar energy system was set when the rain ended in the Sunshine State. The weather radio robot voice reported not much change. It was a little rough, but nothing this boat couldn't take. He was confident his crew could take it, too. His only lament was that they would be under power until they cleared the shoreline and put some distance on. This would use up precious gas. He sat back down and ran his fingers through his hair. A wash of fatigue hit him. He stared out into the rolling water. He thought about all that happened in the past few days. He sat for a minute or two, hearing the comforting sounds of his wife and sons from somewhere below.

The dinghy had suffered some damage. It was still the better choice to take, though, over the Zodiac as the ship's tender. He had been assuming that the Zodiac would stay here, pulled up out of the water onto shore. He had briefly harbored the hope that they could pull it with them. Not in this weather, though, under these conditions. The dinghy was meant to be the ship's tender.

He realized he was overthinking this and wasting time. He stood and grabbed the sliding glass door and stepped out into the windy rain.

Dan looked at the motor on the dinghy and realized the pull cord handle was missing. He reached around back and unlocked the motor cover and pulled it off. As he did, it flipped upside down in his hands and he saw that the emergency pull cord was missing. *Some-*

body, he thought to himself, *knew how to get the motor started despite the broken pull cord.*

He was soon lifting the Zodiac up as high as the quay using Ben's boat winch. He had a very difficult time turning the arm to swing the boat back onto shore but managed. The Zodiac was sitting on the cement. The motor was causing the boat to list slightly to one side. Dan unhooked everything and then tied the Zodiac to some cleats mounted in the cement.

He removed the motor's cover, got some tools, and extracted the handle from the emergency pull cord, replacing the cover when he was done. He cut a piece of rope from the *Caruso* and soon had the pull cord replaced in the dingy. As he worked, he found the emergency pull cord on the floor of the dingy and put it back in its little pouch glued to the top inside of the cover. He put the cover back on the motor, checked the gas level and then started it up. It came to life on the first pull. Satisfied, he hooked up the dinghy to the *Caruso* and winched it into place. He picked up his tools and returned to the Zodiac one last time. He said goodbye to the trusty boat. He doubted he would ever see it again.

Back in the salon, he sat down at the chart table and checked his watch. The tide was turning now. They would be timing things perfectly if they sat for another hour and then started on their way.

Cooper came up the port stairwell into the salon. Dan looked at him for a prolonged second. His little boy almost looked like a man. He was glad Sophie was still so young, his little girl.

"When do we shove off, Dad?"

"Cooper, were you outside or down below?"

"Down below, helping Mom like you asked me to."

"Is Sophie down there with you?"

"No, I thought she was up here with you."

"Tell your mom to stay on the boat no matter what. I am going up to the house."

49

HOSTAGE

Sophie understood that her father was busy. She had asked him to go with her to see Mr. Ben but she never had expected him to say yes. So, she put on her rain poncho, slipped out of the salon, stepped off the *Caruso* and walked to the house. At first she did not think Ben was home. She had knocked but her little hands were not that loud. She pressed her face against the glass doors and cupped her hands around her head to block out the light. She could see into the large kitchen and nobody was there. She was just about to give up, when a large man walked into the kitchen.

Sophie stepped back for a moment, not sure what to do. Did Mr. Ben have a guest? She was about to turn around and return to the boat when the sliding glass door opened. "Hey little girl," said Dog, "do you want to come in?"

Sophie stiffened and asked, "Is Mr. Ben here?"

"Not right now, he's not, but he might be back soon."

"Who are you?"

"Well," Dog chuckled, "I am Ben's friend and I am staying here until he gets back. Who are you?"

"Sophie."

"Sophie, is that your sailboat out there?"

"It's my daddy's," she beamed.

"Do you want to come in, Sophie?"

Sophie turned around and looked back at the boat. Then at Dog.

"You can meet Jillian if you come in."

"Who is Jillian?"

"Jillian is my girlfriend, and she loves to talk with little girls."

"Sure," nodded Sophie as Dog stepped aside. "Why don't you sit down at the table there and I'll find us something sweet to eat."

"Where's Jillian?"

"Taking a little nap but she'll be up soon." Dog opened cupboards.

"What happened to your face?" Dog's hand shot up his cheek and he felt the bruising for himself. As he did so, the wound on his arm was visible to Sophie and she gasped.

"That's why Mr. Ben is letting me stay here," Dog said. "I got in an accident and needed some help." He sat a box of wheat crackers on the table. "Do you like milk?"

"No, not very much."

"Let's see what we have here instead then." He opened up the refrigerator. The gun sat on the top shelf. Dog moved to block her view of the gun. In the small of his back the CZ stuck out, uncovered.

"Why do you have a gun?" Damn, thought Dog to himself.

"Well, just because there are lots of bad people out right now."

"I know," Sophie said with some exaggeration. "My brother shot one and my daddy shot two people."

Dog whirled around in a circle. giving her a can of flavored water. "They did?"

"Yep," she said proudly. "Cooper protected us when we were in the car and Daddy shot two bad guys while I was hiding in the woods."

Dog reflexively looked up at the boat.

"Is your daddy on the boat right now?"

"Yep, and we are leaving pretty soon."

"What's your daddy's name?"

"Dan Littrel and my mom is Kate."

Dog nodded and set another drink down on the table and took a seat.

"Does your daddy know you are up here right now?"

Sophie didn't answer but made a look that conveyed, "I don't know." Dog chuckled.

Dog opened the crackers and spilled a pile out on the table, taking one himself.

"Why did your daddy shoot two people?"

"They were going to hurt my mom."

"Ah," said Dog, "that's a pretty good reason."

"When is Jillian going to get up?"

"I don't know," said Dog, "she's been sleeping a while so it should be pretty soon." He pushed a few crackers her way and continued to question her.

"So do you guys have enough food on the boat? You don't want to be out in the ocean without good things to eat."

"Oh yeah, my daddy plans all of our food. He is really good at sailing, too."

"What does your mom do?"

"She is a physician's assistant which means she is almost like a doctor."

Dog nodded his head. "Wow, that's pretty cool."

"Yep, and she just saved a soldier's life."

"How did she do that?"

"He got shot and she saved him. Right in the road."

This intrigued and worried Dog at the same time.

"Is your daddy in the military?"

"No, but he knows a lot about it. He has guns and stuff."

"Do you mean he has guns on the boat?" Dog asked, leaning in.

"Yep." She said as she crunched a cracker.

"It would be fun to meet your daddy."

"Should I go get him?" she asked with eagerness.

"Naw, not yet," Dog replied casually. "I think it might be better for us to wait until he gets his work done."

Dog lifted out a pail of vanilla ice cream.

"Look what we got here," his eyes twinkled at Sophie as he made a goofy, conspiratorial grin. "We should eat this before anybody else shows up."

She laughed at him and bobbed her head yes.

He pulled out a couple bowls and set them on the table. "Can you scoop these while I go check on something?"

"Sure," she replied cheerfully.

Dog dashed to the entryway. He found the shotgun and checked the breech. Good, a shell was ready for action. He sprinted back and peeked around the corner. Her back was toward him as she struggled with the frozen ice cream. Dog placed the shotgun just around the corner, out of sight but accessible. He walked back into the kitchen.

"Having trouble there?"

She dropped the large spoon in the pail and shrugged. "It's too hard."

Dog sat down next to her, facing the sliding glass doors.

"We'll wait just a minute and it will get soft."

There was movement in the corner of his vision as he looked at Sophie. Somebody was working on the crane at the north end of the cement pad where the *Caruso* was tied up.

"Is that your daddy?"

"Yep," she replied. She sat up in her seat and looked.

"Tell me what you've been doing the last few days."

CONFRONTATION

Dan thought about the door behind him, opening and shutting about an hour beforehand.

"Cooper, I'm going to see Ben, you stay put, okay? Sophie might be up there."

The rain was still steady enough to get on your nerves. He scanned the house for any sign of life. Somebody in the kitchen? He moved faster.

Sophie was sitting at the kitchen table. She was talking and moving her hands. Across from her sat a huge, bearded man. Dan walked straight up to the patio doors. "Hey," he said as he opened the door. He stepped in without an invitation. Dan looked at Sophie, smiling at him, and then across to Dog. The man's face was beaten black and blue. And bloody. He looked tough and Dan immediately felt the danger hanging in the air.

"Hey, Dan." Dog moved one hand toward his back, closer to the handgun.

"Is Ben here?" asked Dan.

"Nope."

"Do you know where he is?"

"Not really," replied Dog.

Dan looked directly as Sophie. "Get back to the boat."

"Whoa, partner," said Dog, sitting forward and reaching across to hold onto Sophie's left arm, "she ain't going anywhere."

Sophie looked at Dan, surprise and fear rimming her eyes.

"Danny boy, sounds to me like you've been a bad boy."

Dan measured his words carefully and said, "Let go of my daughter, we are leaving and don't need any trouble."

"Trouble might have found you, Danny boy." Dog stood and circled around behind Sophie who had started to cry.

"What do you want?"

"Nothing much. Just that sailboat." Dog pointed out behind Dan with his chin.

Dan said nothing. Dog leaned down and wrapped his wounded left arm around Sophie while extracting the handgun from behind his back. He stood back up and pulled Sophie up so she was standing on the chair. Dog flashed the gun from behind his back to Dan, keeping it low and out of Sophie's sight.

"Let her go and I'll stay here," said Dan.

"Hell no, do you think I am stupid? Lay down on the floor and put your hands back up behind your head."

Dan hesitated.

"Now!" screamed Dog. Sophie wailed. As Dan dropped down, Dog backed up, carrying Sophie toward the kitchen entrance. She was kicking and screaming, but Dog held her as if she was a doll. He quickly replaced the handgun in his waistline and hefted the shotgun up with his right hand. He stood over Dan and stuck the barrel of the shotgun on Dan's neck.

Jillian stumbled into the kitchen and stood still, drinking in the scene. She looked down, her mouth open, and then looked up at Dog.

"What are you doing?"

"Shut-up, Jillian," Dog responded.

Dan twisted to one side to see Jillian standing at the doorway.

"Dog, what are you doing? More killing?"

Dog pressed the barrel of the shotgun harder into Dan's neck. Dan flinched.

"Don't move, you bastard!" Dog's voice boomed.

Jillian stamped across the kitchen, and Dog braced for her slap. Instead, she reached for Sophie. Dog allowed her to take her. Sophie buried her face in Jillian's neck and cried, clinging to her.

Stepping back, Jillian glared at Dog.

"What did you think, Jillian? That these rich bastards would let us just walk in here and take it all from them?"

Jillian had an icy stare like a laser beam. "Dog, this isn't right."

"Aw hell, now the stripper is going to tell me what's right and what wrong," Dog sneered.

Jillian set Sophie down in the chair and patted her head. She walked back to Dog and slapped him hard.

Dan saw the CZ stuck in Dog's pants. *How fast could he reach up to pull that gun out and could he knock away the barrel of the shotgun as he did it?*

Dog reached back and grabbed the pistol. With the shotgun in one hand he aimed the pistol at Jillian.

She looked at him through tears. "Do it, be a big man and do it."

They stared at each other for a long fifteen seconds while Sophie continued to sob quietly.

"I am all you got," said Jillian in defiance of the pistol. "And you know it."

Dog let the CZ fall to his side. Dan followed its location with his eyes.

"I need a drink," said Jillian. She opened the refrigerator. Dog saw that Dan had moved a bit more. Dog leaned more weight onto the shotgun.

As he looked back up, Dog saw Jillian. She was holding the gun he had left in the refrigerator. He looked at her with shock at first and then a smile spread across his face.

"You're too chickenshit to do it, Jillian."

"I love you Dog."

The gun blast filled the room. Dog spun as the bullet hit him somewhere on the left side of his head. The shotgun clattered to the floor. Dan rolled out of the way as Dog's huge frame stumbled for a moment and fell backward onto the tile. Dan swooped up Sophie and turned for the door.

As he was crossing the threshold to leave the house he turned back to Jillian.

"Thank you."

She rocked herself with her arms around her own waist, sobs staining her shirt.

He ran toward the boat. Another shot boomed. Dan wondered if he had been hit. He quickened his pace through the pelting rain. Sophie sobbed and shook uncontrollably while Dan cradled her gently.

"Okay, Sophie, it's okay. Take a deep breath and try to slow down a little. It's all okay now." He held her for a moment while she cried. He set her down on the deck of the *Caruso*.

"Tell Mom we are leaving and I want everybody below."

She nodded and ran off, still struggling to gain her composure.

Dan sprinted to the power outlet, opened the box and pried the oversized plug from it. He tossed the cable on board and ran to the water spigot. He unscrewed the hose and tossed it onto the boat. He untied them and threw them onto the foredeck. He did the same thing aft just as the wind began to grip the big boat and pull her away. Dan leaped across the chasm onto her.

Kate threw open the hatch of the salon.

"What the hell is going on?"

"We almost didn't get out of there. There is somebody up there who tried to take Sophie. He held a gun on me. Sophie's okay, but you need to get down there and tie down everything you can."

Without saying a word, Kate turned and went back into the boat.

He looked down at the console. He flipped the power system from shore driven to vessel and turned the key. The dual motors chugged to life. They drifted ten yards out, the wind pushing them fast. With the absence of a deep keel, they moved fast, and it was an advantage in shallow coastal waters like this. Dan slipped her into gear and he angled her around to the south.

He stood behind the wheel, leaning back slightly on the captain's chair. Weather conditions were grim, and Dan wondered if he was making the right decision. They could drop anchor in the Intracoastal away from the mayhem at Ben's house and wait out the worst of the storm. The boat could handle whatever was happening out beyond the inlet, but he wasn't sure if his crew was up for it. The electronic screens glowed green and he reached over to flick on the weather radio. The same computerized voice droned on with the same message.

Kate broke the monotony when she stepped out into the elements to join him. She was wearing a proper rain suit now and looked prepared for anything.

"I am thinking about staying here in the Intracoastal while things settle down out there."

"Please, just get us out of here," she begged, "we can handle the weather."

"The swells outside will be big, maybe 5 to 7 footers, even if the storm is already starting to settle down."

"That big?"

"Big enough to keep me here at the helm for the next ten to fifteen hours. We will probably have to use our engines and that means burning gas."

"You can't sail in it?"

"Sure, I can, but if we get in trouble, we would need to motor sail."

Kate bit her lip. "Where would you tie up?"

"We could just drop the hookup close to the leeward shore." She put her arm around him awkwardly in their all-weather gear and leaned in close.

"I don't want you to stand watch for all that time." She put her head on his shoulder.

He inhaled the salt and rain and then decided.

"Let's just go for it. I won't feel safe until it's just us."

She looked into his eyes. She was about to cry.

"Thanks. Yes, please just get us out of here."

"We'll put up a little sail, not much, and cruise slowly down toward Sebastian Inlet. If we go nice and easy, we can burn off some time while the weather clears."

Up Again

Dog lay motionless on the kitchen floor.

Slowly, his consciousness roused itself. He was alive. He was sleeping, then he was waking. But where? His eyes were wet and sticky and would not open. He reached up and used his shirt to wipe them. He still lay on one side as he looked across the kitchen floor. Jillian was next to him. Lifeless.

Suddenly, remembrance filled his mind. He rolled forward onto his chest and stomach and pushed himself up off the floor onto his hands and knees. His room was spinning. The last thing he had remembered was Jillian pointing a gun toward him. But why? She is laying right there.

His brain tried to process the slow-motion movie events. Was it fifteen minutes earlier? He pushed himself up further, now sitting on his heels with his knees in front of him. He felt a heavy weight on the left side of his head. He raised his hand up and found a large gash. He pulled his hand away. It was iron red.

Somebody shot me, he concluded, *and they must have shot Jillian, too.* He slowly stood as a wave of dizziness washed over him. He placed both hands on the kitchen table and stood for a moment trying to get his bearings. He lifted his head and saw Jillian, grotesquely disfigured.

"Fuckers," he said out loud into the room.

He looked again at her lifeless form, and a deep sorrow filled him.

"Jill, I am so sorry." The dizziness disappeared but emotion gripped him. "I am so sorry."

His head pounded, and a tear carved a rivulet into the blood that soaked his face.

"Those fuckers will pay."

He grabbed the shotgun. He checked the magazine and saw a shiny shell. It was already racked and ready. He turned to the rainy backyard.

The *Caruso* stood off in the middle of the waterway. "Those fuckers have my boat."

His eyes refocused on the Zodiac sitting on the quay.

"They are going to pay."

Dog barreled down the sidewalk, carrying the shotgun. He stopped to wipe bloody rain from his eyes and took off his shirt, wrapping it around his head. His ample belly bounced as he walked. He undid the ropes and pushed the nose of the inflatable toward the edge of the quay. The heavy outboard on the stern was a bigger challenge. He pushed and it barely moved. He got down on his back and put his feet on the rubber gunwale and shoved. The boat moved about two feet. He repositioned and shoved again. The boat tipped over the edge of the cement and disappeared.

Dog realized that he had not tied the boat off.

"Shit!"

He scrambled to his feet and almost passed out. As his vision cleared he saw the boat at an angle, the stern in the water and motor half submerged. The boat's bow was sticking up at a forty-five degree angle. One line had caught on a cleat and kept it from floating free.

Dog fumbled with the rope. He loosened it and let it slip through the cleat. He held onto the end rope and walked the boat down the quay, rain battering his back. He pulled the boat in tight and, gripping the shotgun in one hand, the rope in the other. He descended the cement steps toward the waterline. He crouched into the boat, and it began blowing out to sea.

He pumped the gas bulb, checked the safety switch and pulled the starting cord. He briefly considered the pull cord. Hadn't it been missing? The motor spluttered to life, and he aimed it for the *Caruso* underway toward the south.

He knew these waters. The Indian River, Banana River, the inlets, and outside, the Atlantic. If they were trying to escape to the south, they were most likely heading to Sebastian Inlet. At the rate they were going, he could get ahead and surprise them. There were plenty of hidey-holes around the bridge. Heck, he could tie off on the bridge itself. A big catamaran like that would be no match for the speed of the Zodiac, full on into the wind as it left the protection of the strip of land that created the Intracoastal Waterway. He thought about the tide and the flow of water in and out of the inlet. It could be like a raging river but he could not recall when the tide was turning. He steered to the south and hugged the shoreline. The waves here were minimal here. He risked running aground on oyster beds, but he put some distance between himself and the catamaran.

Dog reached up to feel his wound. His hand jolted. He was touching the bone of his own skull. Everything conspired against him: Jill's death, the weariness of the past few days, the lack of alcohol and the toll of blood loss. The adrenaline that powered him to rise up off the kitchen floor was gone. Now only a depressing heaviness. He felt slow and sluggish.

He turned on the bench to see that the catamaran was almost out of view. It was a mile, maybe two, back and the rain was still falling. He slowed down and wondered if he would make it to Sebastian Inlet at this speed. *Why are they going so slow?*

The motor droned on with Dog occasionally searching for the *Caruso* and then adjusting his speed in front as far as he could.

He was growing inexplicably cold, and he felt short of breath. He dozed but then jerked back to alertness. He looked down at his hands: his fingernails were a strange blue color. In the distance he saw the outcropping of Australian pines and sabal palms that made up the point right before the bridge. He would soon be there. Uncertain if he would make it, Dog turned the handle on the motor and sped off toward the inlet.

51

MAD DASH

The *Caruso* had a roller furled for the mainsail. This was not usual equipment on a catamaran, but Dan was glad for it now. He had purchased the hollowed out boom and inset furler (called a mandrel) from a marine salvage company in Port St. John. Not knowing if his family crew would be much help at sea, he smiled at the ease of the system. He had put out just enough sail to get a little bite of the wind, but not enough to drive them toward any real speed. It was past midday now and despite the rain, the weather seemed to settle down some. The water here was shallow, full of shoals and oyster bars and not passable even for a catamaran. Even with local mariner knowledge, he scanned the charts. Dan was dressed in full rain gear now. He was wearing an inflatable life vest with an integrated safety harness and a black baseball cap with the letters NRA in gold on it. The *Caruso* had standing jacklines meant for the safety line.

Kate delivered a large steaming cup of ramen soup with spices and sauces that tasted like something authentic.

"Thanks, babe," he said to her, "how are the kids doing?"

"I have them busy packing in their gear."

"About fifteen minutes out from the bridge. Once we clear the bridge, you need to be ready for some big wave action."

"Copy that."

"I'll motor through. We could probably do it under sail but no sense risking anything with this wind."

"Need help up here?"

"No, stay dry. But could you send up Kyle? I might need him later tonight."

"No problem. How're you feeling?"

"Great. Going to be a long night, though. Hit the rack early in case I need you later on."

"The kids want to watch a movie on the laptop. We'll bring you some popcorn."

"Sounds great, but you won't be able to make popcorn when we head out. Make sure you tie everything down, babe."

Dan surveyed the boat. From the helm, his world was in order despite the angry sea they'd soon confront. A semi-rigid boat was the only other vessel he had seen. He wondered about the Coast Guard base another inlet further south at Fort Pierce. Would they be out on the water tonight? Probably not in this mess.

"Hey Dad," Kyle popped onto deck.

"What movie are you guys going to watch?"

"Free Willy because Sophie has never seen it."

"Well, you enjoy it. I'll need your help a little later. If I have any problems with the sails I am going to want you right here. Can you be ready for that?"

"Sure, just holler when you need me," said Kyle as he retreated to the cabin.

"Hang on. Take this back down." Dan handed Kyle the empty soup cup. "Give Mom a hug."

Dan set the autopilot for the inlet and clipped onto the jackline. He went forward and checked the furler. All good. As he headed back toward the captain's chair he noticed the dinghy was swinging. He winched it up tighter and added the new line. A few minutes later, Dan turned the ignition switch and could hear the twin motors kick in. He aimed the boat east, directly into the wind as the mainsail flapped. He flipped another switch and the boom furler turned. The big sail lowered itself into the boom. *This feels so good,* he thought to himself. *It is just us, away from the craziness.* The Sebastian Inlet bridge towered before them, red and green channel markers above the black water.

52

FINAL CONFRONTATION

Dog watched from the mangroves as the catamaran's mainsail slid downward. Under his breath he said, "Damn, how does that work?" He had a lot to learn about this vessel. He couldn't hold his head up, and he knew this was his last shot. He grabbed the shotgun and checked the breach one more time. The catamaran was motoring now, so the time was nearing.

His plan was simple. He'd approach the catamaran at full speed and turn off at the last moment. He had found a small anchor and would hurl it onto the boat, locking them together. He would board. He'd kill everybody he found. Vengeance for Jillian.

Dog untied from a mangrove root and prepared the anchor by coiling the rope and chain at his feet. He twisted the handle on the motor and shot out from the mangroves. The distance between the two boats was about 150 yards. Dog was approaching the catamaran from the front, just off the port side. The Zodiac at full throttle could achieve 45 to 50 mph and it was moving now.

Dan sat in the captain's chair as he gazed up at the bridge before him and down at the pilings and timber fenders. He glanced at the console when he heard a motor noise that didn't seem right. He instinctively turned to look at the back of the catamaran when he realized the sound was coming from the bow, not the back. A rigid-hulled inflatable boat aimed directly at them. He pulled back on the throttle. He rubbed the rain out of his eyes and looked again. The oncoming boat was dangerously close to ramming them. Dan turned hard toward the starboard and the boat jogged in the same direction. Dan turned harder to starboard, and jammed down the throttle. They were seconds away from a collision.

Dog bore down on the big multihull. As he did, he slowly stood while picking up the anchor. Like a saltwater cowboy, he swung it around behind him and then flung it as hard as he could toward the catamaran. He fell with a crash to the plywood deck of the Zodiac. His hand scrambled to find the steering handle, and he grabbed it. He pushed it and twisted at the same time. The Zodiac struck the port hull of the *Caruso* in a glancing blow. The big boat bounced from the impact. The anchor had threaded the space between the mast and jib furler. As the inflatable slowed, the rope played out and the anchor caught the safety line running the length of the starboard side. The Zodiac hit the end of the slack and quickly reoriented itself. The *Caruso* was hauling the Zodiac along behind her.

Dan fell off the captain's chair onto all fours on the floor of the cockpit. He was bleeding. He was confused. What had happened? He slowly stood and scanned the horizon; they were heading into the mangroves. He grabbed the wheel and spun it. The boat responded and spun back toward the mainland, away from the bridge. Kyle was shouting, but he ignored it.

As he looked forward, he noticed the Zodiac's anchor line for the first time. His eyes followed it back and then he saw the familiar boat. Standing in the bow was the large bearded maniac from Ben's house. He was pulling on the line hand over hand, shortening the distance. He only had another six or seven feet and he would be up to the *Caruso*.

He's here to kill us.

"Get me a gun, Kyle!" shouted Dan.

They had a few minutes of clear sailing in front of them. He punched the autopilot. He scrambled over to a port side locker and snatched a small hatchet. With his other hand, he lifted a grappling hook on a two-foot pole, normally used to haul large fish onto the deck. He turned to face Dog, who was trying to grab onto the dinghy with one hand while holding a rope in the other. The shotgun was tucked up tight in his armpit.

Dan swung the ax and dropped it on the anchor line. The rope cut like butter and the ax was buried in the deck where Dan left it. He stood as Dog fell forward and heaved up and onto the dinghy. Dog rolled forward and stood, looking down at Dan. The shotgun dropped from his armpit, and he caught it in his open palm. As he brought his finger up to the trigger, Dan leapt into the air with the grappling hook swinging down.

Dan missed Dog but his body came full on and he knocked him down. As Dog fell back, the shotgun blasted a round into the rainy, darkening sky. Dog dropped it and pushed up, propelling Dan up and overboard into the waves.

Dog wrestled with a rope and stood in the dinghy. He reached for the shotgun as Kate appeared on the deck.

"You son of a bitch!" she screamed at Dog, "Where's my husband?"

Dog pointed the shotgun at her chest. Five feet apart.

"You killed Jillian!" he shouted into the wind.

Kate looked with defiance. "We did not kill anybody who wasn't trying to kill us."

Dog lifted the shotgun with one hand. He pulled the trigger.

Above the wind, above the rain, above the din of the two motors and the swishing of ropes, Kate heard a click.

Dog looked down at the shotgun, confused. He racked it, aimed it at Kate, and pulled the trigger again. Click.

Kate lowered herself down to the deck while staring at Dog. Her right hand found the ax sticking up from the deck. She lifted it and it came free.

Dog, looking into the gun's breech, stopped and slowly lifted his face toward Kate.

The hatchet came down squarely in the middle of his forehead.

He fell backward, over the edge of the dinghy. His body hit the water and slipped below for the last time.

Kyle came up behind Kate with an AR-15. She turned to him and yelled, "Stop the boat!"

Dan was being dragged behind the *Caruso* on the safety line. The low-profile flotation jacket had inflated upon hitting the water and the jackline, safety harness and tether had done their job. Kyle pulled his father back up toward the *Caruso*. He was unconscious but breathing. Kate and Kyle pulled him up onto the starboard hull and then onto the cabin deck.

Kyle stood at the helm holding back tears while steering the *Caruso*. Kate sat next to her husband, holding his head in her lap. He blinked to clear the water from his eyes. He tried to talk, but she said, "Hush, my love, we're fine." He looked over and saw Kyle in the captain's seat. To port he could see Cooper walk by with a mooring pole.

"They decided we should take the Zodiac with us," she said, "don't worry, we got this."

FOLLOW-UP

Fifty thousand feet above the surface of the Earth, a Global Hawk drone looked down on Florida's Atlantic coast. Able to see a half-dozen different ways, it was relaying images to a ground-based station in Pensacola in the Panhandle. From there, a digital feed was showing up on a laptop in a makeshift military outpost in Melbourne. Lieutenant Ganoe squinted at the screen, the green light slightly illuminating his face. With the cloud cover the software was doing its best to reconstruct reality, but it took some interpretation to figure out what was happening.

Two red trails lit up on his screen. They were reporting heat signatures, but they were rather odd. They were streaming out from Sebastian Inlet in the middle of the Intracoastal Waterway. They looked like two motorcycles running side by side down a highway.

"Hey," he said to Sergeant Porter, "what do you think this is?"

Porter came over and looked at the screen. "Two boats?"

"Yeah, probably. Hey, could it be a catamaran?" Ganoe looked at Porter.

"I hope so," said Porter, "do you want to call it in?"

Ganoe thought for a moment and said, "Nah, let's leave 'em be."

. . .

IT HAD BEEN MORE than five hours since Officer Raisch had heard anything from her partner and maybe lover Nolan. She was getting worried. Surely he wouldn't leave with her, would he? Her mobile phone rang, and she grabbed it. It was the number from the station.

"Raisch," she said.

"Stacie, Mains," the chief of police identified himself, "When was the last time you saw Nolan?"

She felt a surge of fear go through her body. Were they found out?

"Nolan?" she tried to put him off.

"Yeah, when is the last time you saw Nolan?"

She took a deep breath. She knew lying was a bad idea.

"Last night, why?"

"A forensics team from Melbourne found him dead this morning."

Raisch froze. She squeezed the phone and said nothing.

"A couple of other dead bodies washed up, too."

Still Raisch said nothing.

"Raisch? You there?"

"Yeah, I am. Here. Sir."

"You need to get down here. A detective from Melbourne wants to talk to you. I need some help after that."

"Sure," she hung up the phone. She'd call her mom and ask her to watch her daughter.

DOWN BELOW DAN and Sophie had fallen asleep while Cooper was trying to keep gear from rolling across the boat. Kyle finally shut the motors off, about eight miles straight out from Sebastian Inlet. It was rocking and rolling out here, but the boat was handling beautifully. He let the roller furler put out about one-third of the jib. He knew his dad hated using the gas, and it felt good to turn off the engines. The wind had fallen some, but the swells were still six to seven footers and Kyle wondered how long his dad would be recuperating. Kate stood alongside, both tied in with safety lines.

Kate turned to her son and marveled at how old he was getting.

"I can't make any coffee for you right now."

"Yeah, I know," he said, "it's going to be a long night, too."

"Do you need me to take over for a while?" As Kate said this the boat dropped down the backside of a deep swell.

"The wind will fall off over the next few hours. The wave action might keep up for a while, though. We just put out the jib some. Let's see how she responds and then maybe you can take over."

Kate smiled at Kyle. He gave up a smile the way teenagers do. "Living the life?"

"Yeah," she said, "Livin' the life.

THE END

THANKS AND A FREE STORY

Thanks for reading *Escape, Decide to Survive*. I hope you found it as much fun to read as I did to write it. Reviews are the lifeblood of book sales, and I would appreciate it if you would consider leaving a review for me.

With the advent of the COVID-19 pandemic my traveling has been reduced. I have been hard at work on Book 2, *Voyage*. For readers who want to stay informed about upcoming titles, I produced a short story called *Ghost Scavengers*. It tells the tale of the Littrel's chance encounter with a container ship. Dan thought it was abandoned, but as you find out in this short story, that might not have been the case.

To get a free copy (it is also available on Amazon) sign up for my very occasional newsletter at https://johndeshore.com and you can download it for free.

ABOUT THE AUTHOR

John Deshore is an eyewitness to societal collapse in numerous parts of the world.

From Bosnia, to Syria, Afghanistan and many other hotspots, he has first hand exposure to the brutality that happens when moral controls are wiped away by violence. Deshore has visited over 125 countries, including numerous war zones, sites of pandemic, famine and the inevitable refugee streams they produce.

A lifelong sailor, he brings a unique expertise to the Caruso series.